WITHDRAWN

CORRIGAN'S RANGE

Corrigan—a man of iron with the saving quality of a sense of humor and justice. Corrigan, a rancher who came up against the unscrupulous men who schemed to take over his land and even plotted his death with the help of an inhuman gunman named Hogan.

Not even the burning of his ranch broke his iron will, but then even renegades were marshalled against him ...

This exciting novel is the work of **Norman A. Lazenby** who has written a number of good stories about the legendary days of the Old West under names such as Wes Yancey, John Blaze, Allan Carson and others.

Norman Lazenby has always been intrigued by the rough justice and the hard lives of the early pioneers of the American West. As Jed Norton he weaves these ingredients into a fine drama.

CORRIGAN'S RANGE

Jed Norton

WES
Norton

First published by Robert Hale 1971

This hardback edition 2000
by Chivers Press
by arrangement with the author

© Jed Norton 1971

ISBN 0 7540 8081 1

British Library Cataloguing in Publication Data available

Printed and bound in Great Britain by
Redwood Books, Trowbridge, Wiltshire

Chapter One

He had his hand on the shiny butt of his Colt .45 as he stared at the old line cabin lying about a hundred yards away down the grassy slope. He had seen something move, and these days he reacted to small danger signs with the wariness of a wild animal. In this corner of South Wyoming, near the Green River, he had enemies, particularly the Cassidy brothers, who were increasing their grip on any activity that held the odour of big money.

Big Bill Corrigan, as they called him, always moved with a deceptive slowness. The thighs of his legs were as thick as small trees and that stride could really cover the ground. He walked up to the cabin, his hand soft against his gun.

His horse was standing underneath a big cottonwood, the reins looped over a low branch. He had stopped to rest the wiry brown mustang, roll a cigarette and mull grimly over the past events.

A week ago he had killed a man—one Al Peek, a hot-headed young rannigan in the employ of Sep Cassidy.

5

The encounter had happened in West Plains, right in the heart of the town, with good dependable witnesses to testify that it had been a fair fight. Sep Cassidy, of course, had hollered to high heaven!

Bill Corrigan was not particularly proud of the killing, for to him the other man was a human being with a right to live his life. A conscience, however, was no protection against a fool with a gun. Al Peek had died because he had underestimated Big Bill Corrigan.

He came close to the ramshackle cabin, thought fleetingly that he would have to send a man up to repair the place. Then he paused, pushed his Stetson back, showing a fringe of grey in his thick black hair.

'You there!' he called. 'In the cabin! What are you hidin' for?'

There was no answer, just the whisper of the breeze on this spring morning. Beyond him and all around were the rollings hills and small valleys, green with grass now that the winter snows had gone, and it was all his, Corrigan's Range, if you forgot about a certain amount of mortgage held by the Union Bank in town. Five miles back, in the biggest valley on the spread, lay the ranch-house, a reasonably big building which he had constructed himself from the surrounding stands of timber. The longhorn herd which he had built up was in every valley and fold of the land and pretty soon the branding iron would be busy on the season's fresh crop of dogies. So far everything was going fine for the Double C brand, and maybe Sep Cassidy would consider him too strong to tackle.

6

Bill Corrigan eased the Colt out of the holster and fired a shot into the air. As the echo died away, he yelled : 'You there ! I saw you skulking.'

No answer. He began to wonder if his senses had played him false. Maybe some saddle-tramp was having a night's free lodge. Maybe he should ride on and meet up with Tom Selby as planned.

His thoughts cut with the speed of a twanging Cheyenne arrow and he ducked and rolled flat to the earth as a shot blasted from the edge of the shack door.

He had seen the hand poke around the door frame and he had reacted with a speed amazing in a man of his bulk.

The slug from a handgun dug into the fresh shoots of grass inches from his body. The unknown attacker had tried to follow his dive. Another shot came after the first, but Bill Corrigan was rolling and firing, rolling and firing, as lithe as any Indian.

By the time he had reached the flat wall of the cabin, he had emptied his gun. He breathed hard and refilled the Colt. He saw a wide crack in the planking and he bent down and peered through the slot.

Sure enough he could see the shape of some person inside the square structure, a shape that was flattened to the door frame like a lithe feline. At first it was difficult to distinguish details and then, after a few seconds, one fact at least was evident.

The person inside was a girl!

Corrigan straightened in astonishment and blew down the barrel of his gun. So a girl had tried to ambush

7

him! It would be interesting to find out why! Also, who was she? All he could see through the split planking was an undoubtedly feminine shape in a green blouse and dark skirt.

He looked around the other side of the line shack; wondered where she had hidden her horse. A concealed animal meant that this was premeditated. He saw the clump of cedars standing way back, their trunks thick with a twining berry thicket, and he smiled faintly. The girl's horse must be there. He started to run for the cedars, zig-zagging, jerking, leaping like a half-wit over the grassy slope—anything to throw off a possible shot.

Evidently the unknown girl had not sighted him for he reached the thicket and sure enough a smart little pinto was tethered there. Still breathing fast from the run, he examined the saddle and noticed it was English style to enable a lady to ride side saddle. He saw no brand marks on the pony. He boarded the creature and rode it fast in a wide loop back to the cottonwood where he had hitched his brown mustang. At the last moment the girl evidently sighted him for a rataplan of shots followed him which, at the distance, were woefully wide of the mark.

He hitched the pony to the cottonwood, cupped his hands to his mouth and bawled across the intervening distance.

'Come on out, miss—an' drop that gun!'

Another fusillade of futile shots spurted from the shack. Bill Corrigan shook his head and holstered his gun.

8

'All right, miss, you can walk back to West Plains—
if you've come from there! Or anywhere else! I'm
taking your pony. I don't know who you are or why
you're shootin' at me—but I sure hope you like walkin'!
You just keep goin' south, gal, an' after seven miles you'll
hit town—if that's where you want to be!'

Something like a scream of feminine anger came from
the cabin, and the the girl appeared at the door. The
gun in her hand pointed at the ground. Her breasts
heaved with anger. Raven black hair was tied in a
knot at the back of her head, and now that she was out
in the sunlight he could see that her blouse was bright
green satin and the skirt that fell to her ankles was
dark alpaca.

'Drop that gun,' Bill Corrigan said without anger.

The revolver dropped and she stood. He walked towards her, realizing she was very pretty, with a trim
figure and dark flashing eyes, and probably a foolish filly
—a dangerous one at that! He stopped some yards
away from her—and kept his hand on his gun butt.
It was just habit for he was no gun-fighter, just a
rancher who had learnt to draw fast.

'Now what's the idea takin' me for target practice?'
he asked.

'You're known as Big Bill Corrigan!' she flashed.

'Yup.'

'You killed Albert Peek!' Sudden tears in her eyes
brought confusion to her fury.

'That's right,' he said quietly. 'He came gunnin' for
me—you ask any galoot in West Plains.'

9

'I did. I asked his friends—and they said he was murdered!'

'His friends would say that, miss. You might as well ask Sep Cassidy and Clark Cassidy an' they'd say the same—they hired him to prod me. Now what's it to you?'

'I'm his sister! I hate you! Some day I'll kill you! I've been following you. . . .'

She broke off to wipe her eyes. Bill Corrigan swore softly under his breath and licked suddenly dry lips. He felt dismayed; a little sick at heart that this girl should have been led to the brink of killing a man because of this situation. He hardly knew what to say.

'You've been followin' me!' he mumbled. 'Waal, I didn't see you . . . now look, Miss Peek, I got no argument with you. Why don't you ride into West Plains and see Sheriff Holladay an' he'll tell you the truth about your brother.'

She was sobbing a little. He picked up the gun, emptied the shells to the ground and handed it back to her. She stuck it in her skirt waistband.

'If you like, I'll ride a little way with you,' he said awkwardly.

She changed swiftly like an angry cat. Her hand flashed out and struck his cheek, leaving a red mark on his tanned skin. She ran from him, got her horse and rode furiously away.

Bill Corrigan expelled air between strong teeth and slowly walked to his mustang. He would have to ride on and see Tom Selby.

The bright spring morning playing on the limitless hills suddenly seemed soured and he could not forget the girl. She was young, at least ten years younger than he, and her fury and confused heart-break had left a mark on him. From the moment it had happened he had regretted the killing of Al Peek, but the young fool had forced a showdown. For a long time West Plains had been a law-abiding town and the surrounding territories had been relative free from outlaws, but lately there had been signs that the Cassidy brothers were bringing in trouble-makers, and Bill Corrigan figured that at least two men on the Cassidy payroll were professional gunmen. Something was brewing. Sep and Clark Cassidy were trying to build up an organization which was frankly crooked.

Young Al Peek had just been used, something to be thrown away. Little had he realized that Big Bill Corrigan had faced gun showdowns before, in his wandering days before he had acquired the Double C with a small down payment and a big loan, which was now reduced, and that two men had died before his guns. As a rancher, Bill had hoped his gun-fighting days were over but it seemed the Cassidy brothers were going to alter that.

Sep and Clark Cassidy were not even ranchers; they had moved in with money and were poking their crooked fingers into every established and legitimate business in the area. It was 1878 and this Green River area of Wyoming was, according to the experts, all ready to boom. There was timber and cattle and a branch line of the Wyoming-Utah Railroad was being built. Silver

11

was being mined on the Utah border. Freight wagon lines and stage lines were centred in West Plains. There was even a whiskey distillery in the town. All this spelt money. The demand for labour was at an all time high and strangers were moving into the town, a lot of them drifters without families, and it was from these men that the Cassidy brothers were recruiting.

Bill Corrigan's mustang climbed the last of the grassy ridges and came to the wooded country, thousands of acres of pine interspersed with thickets of juniper, that evergreen prickly shrub with the medicinal berries. It was here that the lumbermen were cutting deeply into the forests and he hoped to meet Tom Selby at his lumber camp to discuss the sale to him of some Conestoga horses.

Tom Selby had talked about buying these large horses for some time, for the hauling of logs, and Bill Corrigan had thought he could help this genial, silver-haired man whom he often met in West Plains. 'These Conestoga hosses,' he had often told Tom, 'are the biggest horses bred an' they can haul a terrific load. I think I know where you can buy some.'

He rode at a canter down the slope into the lumber camp, passed huge stacks of logs and immense wagons. A man waved at Bill Corrigan. Another called out a friendly greeting. Bill soon came to the camp office and he hitched his mustang at the rail. He stared around; caught the smell of pine coming down from the tree-clad hills miles away; heard the thud of axes biting into sappy trunks; not far away a steam-driven saw screamed as it cut into logs.

He opened the office door and stopped dead.

Sep Cassidy's prematurely-wrinkled face stared up inquiringly at Bill Corrigan. Villainy seemed etched into the wreathed lines as he started to grin.

On the other side of the desk Tom Selby sat with his head cupped in his hands. He glanced up but his usual smile was noticeably absent. In fact, for a moment he stared unseeingly at his friend.

It was Sep Cassidy who spoke. 'What the hell d'you want, Corrigan? You've no business here. You're buttin' in on a deal with my pal, Mister Selby, here!'

Chapter Two

Big Bill Corrigan just gave Sep Cassidy the cold stare of a man who is not the slightest bit perturbed. He did think, vaguely, that his own range clothes—black shirt, flapping vest and brown pants—did contrast unfavourably with the other's black store suit, and his battered hat looked terrible compared to the other man's immaculate Stetson, but possibly this was the uniform of a shyster. What was important was the haggard appearance of Tom Selby.

'Say, Tom, what's wrong?' Corrigan narrowed his eyes.

The other made a hapless gesture. 'Nothing—nothing—at all, Bill. I—'

'Don't you feel well?'

'He's fine,' interrupted Sep Cassidy, and he got to his feet and stared insolently at Bill Corrigan.

'You are botherin' him,' said the rancher quietly, 'and what's more you ain't so very big standin' close to me. Why don't you sit down again?'

He put out a hand and just seemed to lean against

Sep Cassidy. The man went down on his seat with a distinct thud.

Corrigan turned to the timber man. 'What's wrong, Tom? Is it this clever jasper?'

'I—I—can't tell you. It's—'

'D'you mind beating it until our business is finished?' Sep Cassidy's sallow face had flushed with anger. 'In fact, don't bother to come back this way again. Mister Selby won't want to see you. You see, we're going to be partners. My brother an' me figure to go into the lumber business.'

Bill Corrigan absorbed this news calmly but inwardly he got the prickly feeling he was dealing with a snake and that there was underhand trickery at work here. Tom Selby would not willingly agree to a business deal with the Cassidy brothers.

'Takin' over needs money,' said Bill slowly.

'We got dough,' sneered the other.

Bill Corrigan walked around the desk. 'Tom, you no more need these jaspers than you need a hole in the head. What are they puttin' over on you?'

The lumberman ran a hand over his face. 'Bill—I'll see you again and—and—we'll have a talk—'

Bill Corrigan went back to Sep Cassidy and looked down at the slick merchant. 'I ought to grab yuh by the collar an' throw yuh down the steps! By heck, I think I will—'

Tom Selby interrupted. 'Bill, that won't do any good. I—I—can't say anythin' more now.'

'What about the Conestoga horses?'

15

'I doubt if I'll be interested!' said Tom Selby harshly.

Big Bill Corrigan nodded. 'All right, Tom. You know where to find me if you need help. But when yuh pick up a snake yuh got to watch yuh don't get bitten!'

With that he left the office building and walked thoughtfully through the lumber-yard. He stopped to talk with a little man in red checked shirt who he knew as a chargehand. 'Sure seem mighty busy here, friend!'

The other grinned. 'Yep. Full steam. Winter's over an' them logs is comin' through mighty fast!'

It was as he thought; the lumber camp was doing fine. There should be no need for Tom Selby to cut the Cassidy brothers in on a business he had worked so hard to build up. Two years ago there had been snags with transportation and a drop in demand, but Tom Selby had got over that. Now, when things were good, he was being persuaded to take in two crooks like Sep and Clark Cassidy. Something was wrong.

In exasperation he stared back at the office. Maybe he ought to go in there and give Sep Cassidy marching orders! That wouldn't be any good, of course, and would not solve the problem. The man might even complain to Judge Hendricks that he was being threatened.

Maybe it would be a good idea to see Judge Hendricks himself and tell him how he thought Tom Selby was being coerced into taking up partners he did not want, but without evidence of trickery what good would that do?

Bill Corrigan finally swung on to his horse and rode out. He could go to West Plains and see Sheriff Dan

16

Holladay but that easy-going man would be little help. Maybe a few inquiries around town might bring forth some information. Jedson the lawyer, for instance, had a nose for news and old Doc Lawson heard a lot of gossip.

On the other hand he had plenty of work to get through back on the ranch—paper-work on his desk, the extension to the bunk-house, branding in the hollows and water-holes to clear of winter's foul. Maybe he should hire another hand.

He went past the line cabin where he had encountered the girl and he smiled faintly in recollection. He wondered where she lived. He had not known Al Peek had a sister. He hoped she would forget her crazy desire for revenge because it just wasn't any good.

At the fork in the trail, he hesitated. Then he figured he would ride into West Plains instead of going east to the Double C. He had not been in town since the gun-fight with Al Peek. He would mosey around and see if he could learn anything connected with Tom Selby's strange behaviour.

West Plains was fairly big and was growing, and he rode past new frame houses going up until he came to an oddity in building planning. A church was being erected on one corner and right opposite a new saloon was being built. A week ago the roof was not on, but now it was complete except for paint and sign-post. It seemed to him that the two edifices were being built in defiance of each other, and he wondered who had sponsored the saloon. The ownership seemed to be a bit of a mystery.

17

He was hungry. He thought inquiries could wait until he had attended to the inner man. He was known in the Broken Horseshoe Saloon, but not as a drinking man. He would have a beer and some steak and maybe hear some news.

He was barely inside the place and seated at a table when he realized the big bearded man at the bar counter was staring in a leering sort of way. Bill glanced up, turned his chair around to that his back was to the man. The lean, mournful waiter brought his steak and fried potatoes. Bill put down his glass and said: 'Walt, who is that rannigan—the one with the beard like a mountain bear.'

'Stranger, I guess. Maybe he's an Irishman seeing he's wearin' that round hard hat.'

'Yep. Could be. Seems to me he's had too much hooch.'

Bill Corrigan tackled his steak, which was running with appetizing juices and flopping over the sides of the plate. He was hungry and food wasn't just a habit; it was something he needed.

The saloon had a scattering of men at the bar and tables and there were two Bill knew fairly well. He waved a fork to them and grinned.

The bearded man sauntered from the bar, came round the other side of Corrigan's table, turned a chair and sat on it the wrong way, his arms folded on the chair back. He leered at Corrigan, his lips an unpleasant red through the blackness of his beard. Bill Corrigan ran his eyes over the man, noted the gun in the belt, no holster

18

but all set for a left hand draw. The man was fairly big in tight check pants and a yellow shirt and a checked vest.

'You hungry, curious or what, pal?' asked Bill. 'Or maybe you just don't believe in manners!'

The man laughed derisively. 'Now isn't the boyo gettin' mighty fussy about the company he keeps! A man might think the high an' mighty Mister Corrigan would go to the classy eating-house down the street.'

'I like the steaks here. Seems yuh know me?'

'Yup. Yuh're the boyo who gits away with murder in this town.'

Bill Corrigan put down his knife and fork. He stared at the steak and said: 'I'll give yuh half-a-minute to git the hell away from me!'

'I like it here,' said the other insolently, but Corrigan noticed he was suddenly sitting taut on the wood seat.

Corrigan jumped to his feet, really angry but at the same time controlled. The bearded man rose more slowly and they faced each other.

'The half-minute is up,' said Corrigan.

Both men went for a fast draw as if mind-reading. Inside a split second the bearded man found himself staring at the black hole in Corrigan's Colt while he was in the act of tugging his gun from his trouser belt. He froze instantly.

'Yuh're not good enough, hombre,' said Bill Corrigan. 'The galoot who told yuh to go for me should have told yuh it's dangerous work. Now jest drop that gun nice an' easy.'

19

The leering smile was noticeably absent as the man did as he was told. Surprise had narrowed his eyes to mere slits. The revolver hit the wood floor. Men at the bar took in deep breaths. The barkeep was still reaching for his shotgun. Walt, the waiter, trembled in a corner.

Bill Corrigan unbuckled his gunbelt and it hit the floor with a soft thud. He stared at the other man.

'I could have killed yuh—but maybe that's what somebody wanted me to do. I'd have had witnesses to prove a fair fight but I reckon another killin' wouldn't look so good in this town. Still, maybe yuh're as good with your fists as yuh are with your mouth!'

Both men struck out, not lacking in fast reactions and anxious to get in with the first punch. In fact, both men landed blows and Bill Corrigan knew the Irishman could fight well enough. The man's derby hat went spinning. His bearded face twisted into a fighter's mask.

At first the exchange of blows was typical of the times —a good stand-up punching session, with punch and counter-punch and little movement of the feet. Then it inevitably became a rough-house as the bearded man tried to hook an arm around Corrigan's neck.

A nasty jab came up into Corrigan's stomach as he got out of the neck hook, but it met with hard muscles although it was pretty low down. Corrigan grabbed the man's arm, twisted it and forced him towards the bat-wings. Reaching the swinging doors, they battled through and hit the boardwalk outside. Corrigan slammed the other man to the hard earth; then crouched with upraised fists and waited for the other man to rush in to the attack. To give the Irishman his due, he came back for more. He got it in the form of two deadly blows that smashed through his flailing fists and landed with first-class accuracy on the chin and nose. Blood instantly spurted and dyed the black beard. The man spat, came on again. He had not hurt Corrigan and his attack this time was not quite so impetuous.

They moved from the boardwalk to the hard earth road, struggling like wrestlers and then rough-housing with gutsy punches. Corrigan was unmarked although he had been hit a few times. The other was worse for wear. Both eyes were bruised and would undoubtedly close up and give their owner a painful reminder for some time to come. Corrigan hit him hard again, penetrating the thrashing arms at the right moment, and the man went down to the ground.

Bill figured it was time to end the show. People had gathered for the free entertainment, grinning cow waddies, wagon drivers, drifters, rail-road workers and disapproving women. He picked the other man up boldly.

Without any outstanding effort, he carried the struggling man to the horse-trough outside the saloon and neatly dropped him in!

'Cool off, durn yuh!'

There was some laughter and the crowd dispersed except for one man who stared without amusement. He was a handsome fellow in a large black hat, store suit and gold watch-chain. He carried a leather valise with the initials E.H. He watched Bill Corrigan re-enter the Broken Horseshoe Saloon, glanced at the bearded man as he climbed dazedly out of the trough and then went into the saloon.

Bill was staring grimly at his unfinished steak and buckling on his gun-belt when the man walked up.

'You handled that pretty well, friend,' said the stranger.

'Yeah. But it spoilt my dinner.'

'Who do you work for?'

Bill stared. 'I don't work for any one, mister. I'm a rancher.'

'Sorry. I figured you might be a strong man for some people in this town. What I want to say is—I'm looking for two men called Cassidy. Clark Cassidy and his brother Sep. Would you know where I could find them? I've just got off the Overland Stage.'

'What the hell d'yuh want with them?' demanded Bill Corrigan.

The other man gave a placating smile. 'I am going to work for the Cassidy brothers, friend. A sort of manager to their many business interests. My name is Ed Hunter —from Montana.'

Bill Corrigan said roughly: 'You'd better go look for the Cassidy galoots yourself, pal. Right now I'm kinda fed up with those two. I reckon they hired that jasper I put in the trough to prod me—so if yuh aim to be pally with them Cassidy men please keep out o' my way, Mister Hunter.'

'I'll bear that in mind,' said the other man mildly. 'Thanks for the information. I'll locate the Cassidys myself.'

He went to the bar and ordered a whisky. He watched Bill Corrigan thoughtfully through the mirror at the back of the bar and then, after downing his drink smiled and left the place. Bill glanced up as the man left and wondered just how he would fit in with the Cassidy schemes. He was certainly no gunman but there was a shrewd brain behind that smiling countenance.

Bill Corrigan had an irksome feeling that he should be back at the Double C and attending to his own work instead of moseying around town. All the same he would like to help Tom Selby, because they had been friends. Maybe he should go along and look up old Doc Lawson. That talkative old cuss always knew something about somebody!

As luck would have it he found the doctor at his surgery, sitting at a battered old desk and reading a week-old newspaper. Doc Lawson looked up and smiled. He smoothed down his stained vest and tugged at his coat lapels and tried to look dignified—at which task he failed because he resembled a white-haired little gnome!

'I've been to see Tom Selby up at his camp,' said Bill going straight to the point. 'And I'm worried about him.'

'Well, now, what's his trouble?' asked Doc Lawson eagerly. 'I can't prescribe without seein' the patient— an' I always figured Tom was a mighty healthy man ... still you never know ... how are you yourself ... fine maybe, huh? Guess you're too tough. ...'

'Whoa, Doc! I'm fine. It's Tom—an' it isn't his health. Look, he's mixed up with the Cassidys. ...' And

23

Bill Corrigan told the gabby old doctor as much as he knew.

'Tom Selby, huh?' murmured Doc Lawson. 'And them twisting Cassidy boys—oil and water don't mix! You know Tom Selby only came to this territory about four—five years ago . . . guess we don't know everything about a man . . . though I'd say he was a straight-shootin' feller . . . say, you know I'm supposed to respect people's confidences!'

'Sure, Doc.' Bill smiled. 'But we're tryin' to help Tom Selby. Waal, it seems it's a mystery how come those two crooks can horn in on Tom's business like this. Guess I'll mosey along and attend to my own affairs!'

He rode out of West Plains thinking it was true that most people in the area had not known Tom Selby for very long but then this was true of many men and certainly applied to the Cassidy brothers. Anyway, he wouldn't forget Tom. And he would find out something about the setup somehow.

As Bill Corrigan rode down the main stem, tall in the saddle on the wiry mustang, he was observed from an office window. In a white-painted building that had once been a draper's store, Clark Cassidy watched the big man ride slowly past the window and then he turned.

'Now there's a man we'll have to watch,' he said.

'I've met him already,' said the man known as Ed Hunter. 'He's seemingly a resolute character.'

'We'll smash him!' said Clark Cassidy. He was a smallish man with cold blue eyes and thin hair. He had a clean-shaven baby-like face which was so deceptive because it hid a brain like a calculating machine. He was, in fact, the power behind his brother. Clark Cassidy dressed like a bank clerk and he had never worn a gun-belt in his life, but few people knew that he carried a small derringer in a special pocket inside his jacket. He had never used it in West Plains. Only Sep Cassidy knew that the small gun had been used elsewhere and that two men had died by the hand of this deceptive man.

'Corrigan handled a tough jasper in the saloon,' said Ed Hunter reflectively.

'Hmm, that man wasn't much use,' said Clark Cassidy, 'But he might easily kill Corrigan some time—probably a shot in the back if I know the man.'

'You really want to eliminate Corrigan?'

'Yes. He had an instinctive desire to oppose us—and that's a nuisance—but apart from that Sep and I think that ranch of his could be profitable.' Clark Cassidy lowered his blue eyes; put his finger-tips together as if discussing some academic problem. 'This town is ripe for centralization of financial interests, but these chances don't just fall into our hands—we have to give them a push. You will assist in this work, Mr Hunter—mainly in business matters. We can hire strong men. Gun-men are plentiful, too. With a bit of luck we will build a business empire here.'

'Why did you select West Plains?' asked Ed Hunter mildly.

'If you must know we operated for a time elsewhere

but it failed. We—er—had to leave. But one learns from mistakes. This time we will not fail. We will take over—but always at our price—always on our terms—until we are masters of this area.'

'Good,' said the man known as Ed Hunter. 'I'll be at your service. Now I must find somewhere to stay.'

An hour later he was in a hotel room. He had finished washing at the dresser, using the china jug of hot water, and his jacket was carefully draped around a chair.

Around his body was a leather harness and in a holster near his left armpit lay a small, neat revolver which was not very bulky. He finished dressing and put on his jacket very carefully. He went to the window and stared across the street at the Cassidy brothers' office.

At that moment Ed Hunter did not look like a mild-mannered businessman.

Big Bill Corrigan put the mustang to a fast canter as he left West Plains behind. He took the trail east to the Double C, seeing the signs of activity all around. Two freight wagons were lumbering towards the town; in a grassy hollow a small herd was resting, probably waiting a cattle buyer. He grinned, kicked the horse's flanks. He wanted to get home.

Home to him was the rolling grassy hills of the Double C, the smell of cattle, the neat layout of horse corrals, barns and buildings, the odour of grub as Li Foo did his best or his worst according to mood, the warmth of summer and the piercing snow storms of winter. This was home.

He was two miles from the ranch, riding along a grassy ravine, when the attempt at ambush came. He was taken by surprise. It was a rifle shot that rang out from the top of the ridge. The bullet missed him by less than an inch, tugging at his shirt, and then buried itself in the horse's neck.

The animal jerked wildly, showed its teeth in agony and then stumbled to its knees. As the second shot rang out, Bill Corrigan threw himself sideways from the saddle, legs kicking free of the stirrups. The horse leaped up and ran a few yards and then fell again, kicking as if half paralyzed. Bill flattened in some long grass, his gun in his hand. A third shot cracked from the ridge and the slug bit into soil near his face. Not waiting for the next shot, which might be more accurate, he rolled swiftly to a new spot which was a hole in the ground that might have afforded cover to a jackrabbit. Another shot attempted to get him and once more dug into earth. He flung a desperate shot at the ridge and again hugged the ground like a cowering canine.

The mustang was lying on its side, kicking crazily and giving shrill whinnying sounds. He wished he could put the animal out of its misery but he half-expected a slug in his own hide any moment. He lay still, as if dead, and did not even twitch when another bullet bit dully into earth only inches from his outstretched arm.

This old Indian trick required nerve and was not always successful but a man ambushed and out in the open hasn't many tricks to call on. He played possum. He lay as if dead.

27

For a moment there was silence from the ridge as if the attacker was considering the situation. Then, ear to the ground, listening intently, Bill heard the sounds of boots slowly clumping over hard earth. The man was walking nearer.

Just to lie without twitching, motionless, and with all other senses vibrating on a high level of alertness was an ordeal in itself. One mistake in timing and the attacker would still win. He lay with his hand inches from his gun as if it had fallen from his grasp. He thought he could reach it and fire when the time came faster than hell's own! The moment was almost at hand . . . now!

It was a simple but deadly trick. He whipped into action with every instinct for self-preservation blazing in his mind, and his hand slapped down to the gun and jerked it into line with the oncoming man in less than a second.

The Colt .45 gave its characteristic roar. The slug hit into the man and halted him instantly. The man's rifle dropped to the ground and he staggered back. Once more the Colt barked, because Bill Corrigan was not playing games, and the second slug drilled the man's head. As he fell heavily, he was dead.

Bill Corrigan stared at the bearded face, the checked pants and yellow shirt. The man's round derby hat lay to one side. For a moment Bill Corrigan was sickened. In death this man just looked pathetic, a bundle of rags lying in an unnatural position, with trickling blood the only sign that once there had been life.

Then he realized that he, too, could have been the crumpled object on the ground, staining the earth, and he swore and got to his feet and stared again at the man who had tried to kill him. So the duped fool had decided to have another go, the drygulcher's way, in order to earn his money? As the man could have no personal enmity, it was obvious who had financed his mission.

Bill wasted no more time. He went to his writhing mustang and finished the animal's life with a slug in the head. He then scouted around until he found the Irishman's nag.

He hoisted the man on to the saddle, tied him in position with the rope he found there, and then sent the cayuse off with a slap to the flanks. He was probably right in thinking the horse would trot back to West Plains, and the corpse would tell its own story to whoever was interested.

He set off walking. The exercise cleared his thoughts and presented one dominating point: in seven days he had been forced into killing two men, dupes of the Cassidy brothers. The role of gunman was not one he liked but at least he was alive. All the same the 'killer' tag had a nasty habit of sticking and there might be folks in town who might wonder why he had to resort to the gun.

When he reached the ranch, he strode past old Bert Foggin, his leading hand, in a very grim mood. Bill shouted to Li Foo that he wanted hot water and soap. He wanted a bath.

He came out later in a better frame of mind and talked to the old-timer in the ranch-yard.

'I've just had a shootin' ruckus, Bert,' he said, 'and I figure Sep Cassidy was behind it—an' his brother!'

'Yuh shore look in one piece to me!' cackled Bert Foggin. 'So I reckon the other galoot got it.'

'He did,' said Bill. 'But I didn't leave him for buzzard bait—I sent him back to town on his hoss. Maybe the Cassidys will get the message. And while I think, send a hand out to collect my saddle off'n that mustang before some range tramp picks it up.'

'Shore, boss. Say, mebbe tomorrow we kin ride round by the Green River an' git a branding party started.'

Bill grinned down at the whiskery old man. 'Yep, we'll start at sunup. Say, d'yuh ever sit down, Bert?'

'Not iffen I kin help it! Say, I ain't old! I jest look kinda old—an' iffen I start sittin' around folks might think I'm dyin'!'

'You do more than your share around here, Bert.' And Bill Corrigan smiled and returned to the ranch-house and went to his desk.

He was busy for some time and then he did some work on the bunk-house extension. Just before sundown his two hands came in with news of the herds in the hills. A bit later he returned to the ranch-house and studied plans to extend it. He was, in fact, running only a middle-size spread and he could grow bigger.

He stared out of the window at the gathering dusk and felt the return of the old lonely feeling. Maybe he should be married, with a woman about this house, because something seemed lacking. Of course, he could have been in town, hitting a bottle with some pals and may be chatting up a saloon girl but, in actual fact, he indulged in little for that kind of life. Still, maybe a man should relax now and then. . . .

Much later he was in bed, doors locked and barred, the black mongrel dog in his outhouse. The hands had evidently quit playing cards and were silent in the bunk-house. Only the wind sighed and a half-moon shed its radiance. He fell asleep.

When he did waken it was fast, instant, with the jarring knowledge that something was wrong and that the night was still young. The dog was barking wildly and, simultaneously he heard the flurry of horses's hoofs. Then there was some curious dull thuds on the roof. He leaped out of bed, scooped up a gun and went to the window. He saw two horsemen disappearing in the night, through the open ranch-yard gate, and the dog was howling defiance.

He threw fast slugs at the riders but it was a forlorn hope of hitting them. Then he was aware of the smell drifting in the window—of burning tar and wood—and he knew they had fired the ranch-house roof.

Chapter Three

Bill Corrigan was dressed and out of the house as fast as any man could do it. Shirt, pants, gun-belt and boots —he was ready. The two riders had gone into the night, but they had already done their evil work.

The roof blazed already, with the tar torches burning fiercely into the wood shingles. And somewhere at the back of the ranch-house he discovered they had started two more fires against the wall. He stamped into these fires, boots kicking and stamping, with a fury as livid as the flames. He bawled instructions to the hands who had appeared sleep-eyed at the bunk-house porch. They ran back, grabbed buckets, went to the well and the horse troughs, passed them along to Bill Corrigan. He grabbed a long ladder, set it up the side of the ranch-house, shouted to the men to pass the buckets. He aimed the water with grim accuracy at the burning patches, threw the buckets back to the ground and grabbed at more as they were passed up, but it was a futile counter-attack to the hissing flames. The cedarwood shingles, with which the roof was covered, were well alight.

There was not enough water coming up to him and he shouted angrily for someone to work the well pump faster. It was no good, however, and the supply of water could not be hurried. The tar from the torches was running in blazing rivulets down the roof, pausing here and there to eat into the cedar with swirling red fingers. Sparks crackled into the air and hot flames wafted sullenly into his face as if the building was suddenly antagonistic. He breathed smoke and the devilish fire; threw water frantically and saw it turn almost instantly to protesting steam.

Then a portion of the roof fell inwards with a triumphant roar and sparks flew madly. The futile water sloshed foolishly again and again, directed by a grim man on a jerking ladder. The hands below shouted their dismay and warnings, but Bill Corrigan fought on and on, bawling curses when the buckets did not appear quick enough. His face was a mask now, blackened and desperate, alternately glaring at his men and then at the sea of fire before him.

And then it was hopeless and even he saw failure to halt the holocaust. The roof was falling inside the house and adding to the inferno.

'Get things out of the house!' he croaked and slid down the ladder.

He was the first to dash inside and grab at a few personal belongings—papers from inside his desk, clothes, a rifle. He rushed out, head down, eating smoke and wood ash. He collided with old Berg Foggin and halted him.

33

B

'You ain't goin' in there!' he choked. 'Stay out! I'll do it!'

'Hell, I got to burn someday!' yelled the old-timer. 'Might as well see what it's like!'

'You keep out, yuh old fool!'

The crackle of burning timber was now a victorious sound and the fire danced in reddish elation. Old Bert Foggin ran into the house wearing pants, braces, flannel undershirt and boots. He seemed to vanish in the flames and a gust of black smoke belched leeringly. Bill Corrigan threw a bucket of water over his head and, spitting, went back into the fire.

Immediately, the smoke and flames choked him, like an assassin's hands. He could not see. He had in mind to get pictures of his mother and father from a mantelshelf, but a fit of coughing doubled him. Then, with new alarm, he wondered what had happened to Bert Foggin.

This living-room that he had once known as home was now a strange world of eddying flames and smoke and he hardly knew which way to turn. There was a back door; maybe old Bert had gone out that way.

A chunk of red-hot sparring crashed on to the back of his neck and sent him staggering. He straightened, clawed his way across the room, towards the kitchen door. He stumbled over something and knew it was Bert Foggin, face down on the floor. Something had happened to the oldster. Maybe he had been overcome by the smoke or may be he had been hit on the head by a falling beam. Right there and then he was unconscious.

34

He had to get out of this insane inferno; get into air where he could breathe, away from this red-hot menace around him. He bent down, grabbed the old-ster, hoisted him on to his back and felt sudden heat sear his eyeballs. He fought a panic to run this way and that way, anything to dodge the devilish fires that flared at him. He had to go straight through a wall of fire to the door. He had to! His boots dug at the littered floor as he shot forward. The seconds of sucking fire and ash seemed an age—and then he was free and the cool night air ran into his throat with a sob.

He sank to the ground with the old man. One of the hands sloshed a bucket of water over them.

'Yuh're burning, Mister Corrigan!'

The cold water did more than damp out charred clothing; it revived him and even old Bert Foggin stirred and spluttered.

Bill Corrigan got up again and stared at the ruins of his ranch-house. Months of work, money and pos-sessions that meant a lot to him had gone—blasted into ash and smoke by two unknown riders. He knew, with-out any analysis, just who was responsible for this body blow.

The Cassidys!

Money could hire ruffians and they had done just that. So this was war!

Staring at the blazing remnants of his home was no good. One of the hands had got the horses clear of the stables and they were now in a safe corral. The barn was safe. He strode furiously around to see if any flying spark had settled near the bunk-house or the workshop. It was a good thing the Double C buildings were widely spaced. The rest of the place seemed all right.

Hours later where the neat little ranch-house had stood there were only charred, blackened timbers that smouldered sullenly. There was little sleep that night for the men of the Double C. and sunup found them bleary-eyed and trying to rest in the bunk-house. Bill Corrigan lay flat on a bunk and stared at the roof, speaking to no one for a long time.

It was Li Foo who attempted to bring back normality to the others. On an old range in the bunk-house he cooked a hefty breakfast consisting of bacon and beans and coffee, and began to dish it out on the few tin plates he could find.

Bill Corrigan ate slowly, stowing the grub away as if it was a reserve of strength. Then he stripped and washed in the yards with cold water and lye soap. He shaved determinedly. He borrowed clothes off Sam Hicks, one of the hands who was about his size. Guns had been rescued from the rifle case in the ranch-house, and he examined a Winchester and then his colt .45. He took plenty of ammunition for the guns. This was stored in the bunk-house for the hands' use. He saddled a horse from the corral and stuck the Winchester into the big holster. Then he got into the saddle.

'I'm goin' into town to buy me a new Stetson,' he said.

'Yeah?'

'And see some mangy polecats,' he said grimly.

'Want me to come, boss?' rapped Bert Foggin.

'Nope. Stick around an' find work to do. Keep yore guns handy. Any strangers ride up, start shootin' if they don't talk sense fast. When I git back we'll start on clearin' the ranch-house site. I might hire me a carpenter an' buy some lumber. We're building the ranch-house again—just like it was.'

He put the fresh horse to a fast canter and took the easy trail to West Plains. The spring morning cleared his head and he forgot about his lack of sleep. It was not the first time he had missed a night's shut-eye.

Two hours later he entered the town, one man among many hundred others all intent upon their business.

He rode first to the Sheriff's office and tied his horse. He went inside and found the sheriff with his feet up, drinking coffee. Dan Holladay dropped his feet with a guilty start and smiled at Bill.

'Hi! How's it go, Bill? Hear you've bin havin' trouble.'

'What sort of trouble, Dan?' The rancher stared grimly.

'That Irish feller . . . horse brought him in . . . dead . . . last night. . . .'

'Yeah? You figure I killed him?'

'Yuh had a fight with him—'

'All right, I killed him. Want to know? He tried to bushwhack me on the trail home. I can show yuh the spot an' maybe yuh'll find spent shells. That should clear me.'

'I guess you're in the clear,' said the sheriff hurriedly.

He was a man of medium height, of no ambitions and a careful desire to please everybody. He was in his early thirties, with thinning hair and a large moustache.

'Yep—in the clear,' snapped Bill. 'Well, listen—some guys burnt down my ranch-house last night. Two riders with tar torches. If I find them you'll have two more corpses. As it is I can guess who hired them to do the job—the Cassidy brothers.'

'You've got to prove that,' said the sheriff carefully. 'Cassidys! Hell, that's a serious accusation, Bill.'

'They paid the Irish jasper, too.'

'Now, look, you've got to be mighty careful sayin' things like that,' said the other protestingly.

'I know what I'm saying'. Ever since Sep Cassidy rode into my ranch-yard and had the gall to offer to buy me out an' throw out hints as to what might happen if I didn't accept. An' who stirred young Al Peek into gunnin' for me? An' the Irish feller? Who is puttin' the pressure on Tom Selby, I know—if you don't know, Sheriff Holladay!'

'You've got to have proof,' insisted the other. His face was white with worry.

'Yeah? Maybe I'll git it!' And Bill Corrigan strode out, slamming the door behind him.

His next call was at the white-painted office belonging to the Cassidy brothers. He went in with a rush that nearly tore the door off its hinges. With no more respect he opened another door that led to an inner office and smiled with grim satisfaction as Sep and Clark Cassidy looked up.

38

'Fine. Seems I got the two of yuh together for once! Your dirty night riders made a good job of my ranch-house.'

'Get out of here!' Sep Cassidy rose to his feet, his wrinkled visage sneering. 'We don't know what you're talking about.'

'I think I'll give the two of yuh a damn good hidin'!' retorted Bill. 'That's fair odds, ain't it? Two half-men to one! Unless you care to grab a gun an' git out in the street!'

'There is law around here—'

'Not enough. So I'll give yuh a hidin'. And every time yuh figure to cross me in future I'll come back an' give you hell again. That should sicken you two carrion.'

Bill reached out and grabbed the two men by the collar, a hand for each man. He rammed their heads together and heard their snarls of pain.

Then he froze as a door at the back opened and a tall thin man with twin guns pointed them with obvious skill at his heart.

'Raise your hands, feller. Go for that gun an' you're dead!'

The man's thin features were like a ferret. His black glittering eyes were ready for the slightest wrong move. Bill Corrigan backed away and slowly took his palms up to his shoulder level. This twin-gun man had killer written all over him, in the thonged down holsters, the white hands so carefully manicured and the nervy tautness of his thin mouth. His pants, shirt and hat were

39

black and seemed to accentuate the whiteness of his face.

'You have the better of me, hombre,' Bill murmured. 'But then you kinda appeared unexpected.'

The man jerked a glance at Sep Cassidy. 'This the guy that's botherin' you, boss?'

'We're bothering him!' sneered Sep. 'He'll be glad to come to terms pretty soon.'

Clark Cassidy rubbed his head and grimaced with pain. 'Heavy-handed swine! You'll suffer for this!'

'I c'd blast him,' said the gunman unemotionally.

'Not here,' said Clark quickly. 'It might not look so good. He has friends. But anytime you fancy your guns against his, Hogan—and you can choose the time and place—we'd laugh to hear he's bitten the dust.'

The black eyes flicked again. 'I got room for another notch.'

Bill Corrigan laughed in the man's face. 'Which owl-hoot trail did yuh ride down, feller?'

The guns stared, two round holes in black metal. The white hands did not waver. Above that the pale face looked at Bill Corrigan as if memorising every detail.

'Yuh won't ride back,' said Bill brutally. 'We got a good undertaker in West Plains.'

He turned his back and walked from the office. He went through the open door, into the outer part of the building and into the street. Only then did he expel air from his lips. So that was one of the Cassidys's bodyguards! A twin gun-hand! He did not doubt the man had speed and nerve to match his hardware.

He had taken a chance in turning his back. Maybe the gunman might take pride in a fair fight, but Sep Cassidy wanted him dead as long as there was no kick coming to him. He had hinted to this man, Hogan, that he could choose his own time for the showdown.

Bill Corrigan instinctively loosened the Colt in his holster. He lounged against a tie-rail and watched the white-painted office. He remembered when it had been a draper's store and doing reasonably well. The man and wife owning it had sold out to the Cassidys pretty quickly. Then they had left town. It was a good guess they had been threatened and had to sell at a bare-faced robbery price.

Looking at the property, built mostly of timber, it seemed there was an obvious reprisal. The Cassidy brothers had fired his ranch-house; he could fire their office!

They had sent men like curs at night. Men he did not know. It would be nice to discover the identities of these hired desperadoes. It seemed he would have to fight the Cassidys himself because Sheriff Holladay seemed disinclined to take any action.

He walked along to the Broken Horseshoe Saloon and thought he would talk to Walt, the waiter. He went inside and sat down and beckoned the nervous man over.

'Will you bring me a beer, Walt—and have one yourself.'

'Sure, Mister Corrigan.' The man hurried away and presently returned with two glasses. 'Heerd about that

41

feller yuh fought with yesterday. Seems he got filled wi'
lead somewheres out in the grasslands.'

'Hear anythin' else, Walt?'

'Such as?' The waiter's eyes could not meet his. He
was a bundle of nerves. If someone had said 'Boo!',
he'd have jumped a mile!

'Such as my ranch-house bein' burnt down last night,
Walt.' Bill watched him coolly.

'Burnt down!' The man seemed to gulp.

'Burnt, Walt.' said Corrigan harshly. 'To a durned
cinder. By two night riders.'

'Two riders!' echoed Walt. He grabbed his beer and
gulped at it. 'Now—now—who the heck would ha'
done a thing like that to a gent like yuh, Mister Corrigan?'

'That's what I'd like to find out,' said Bill. 'And yuh
seem to overhear a lot o' little snatches o' conversation
in a place like this, don't yuh, Walt.'

'Well, mebbes . . .'

'No maybe about it. You come up with something
definite, Walt—you know, like how some two gents
were out ridin' last night—or maybe boastin' about
raisin' fires—or maybe jest mentioning my name—any
little thing, and I'll be disposed to drop yuh about twenty
dollars if it's good.'

'Twenty dollars!' stammered the man. 'More'n a
month's pay! I—I—I'll see—maybe I'll hear somethin'.'

'Fine.' Bill Corrigan rose. 'I'll be here again.'

The role of the informer was always a harrowing one,
he supposed, and he had no scruples about using the

man if it meant discovering the identities of the two men who had actually taken Cassidy's orders and fired the place.

Because those two men would pay for their crime.

Bill Corrigan stepped through the batwings, determined to stir up more grief for the Cassidys, and almost bumped into a passing lady. He apologized and then looked into dark flashing eyes.

They belonged to the girl who was the dead Al Peek's sister!

The recognition was mutual but hardly pleasant. She backed from him, not because of fear apparently, but with some sort of loathing. It was a reaction he did not like. She stared with mounting anger, and he realized once again she was a dark-haired flashing beauty. She wore a dark dress, embroidered, with a tight waist, and her hair was done in a neat coiffure.

'You!' she breathed. 'You strut around this town—' She broke off.

'Miss Peek, I do not strut,' he began, 'and believe me I am sorry for any trouble I have caused you—'

'You have killed another man!' she interrupted. 'I have heard about that, too. You seem—'

'It was self-defence,' he snapped. 'Have you heard that, too, Miss Peek? Or are you so busy building up a hate for me? An' maybe yuh've heard about my ranch-house bein' fired? No? Maybe I can tell yuh, then—or don't yuh want to listen.'

'I'm not interested. In fact, I'm glad. Glad! You've

43

only lost a ranch-house—I lost a wonderful brother! He was all I had.'

'This is a frontier town,' said Bill harshly. 'A man carries a gun to save his hide. Young Al Peek came gunnin' for me. He was full of bravado and cheap whisky. He taunted me in front of witnesses. I wouldn't ha' drawn a hogleg even on that, but he cleared leather. It happened fast, believe me—an' then he was dead. Would yuh rather I died without defendin' myself? If yuh really want to hate somebody start findin' out who sent your brother gunnin' for me. I kin tell yuh—I discovered he was in an' out of the Cassidy office days before the shootin'. Ask a few questions, Miss Peek—or don't yuh belong around here?'

'I lived in Laramie,' she jerked. 'I'm a teacher. I came to West Plains after Albert—died—'

'Go back,' he said grimly. 'There's nothin' yuh can do now.'

She lowered her eyes. Confusedly she said: 'I made a—a vow—I said—I'd have revenge—'

'Killin' me would do yuh no good,' he said quietly. 'Yuh can use a handgun apparently—but have yuh ever seen a person lyin' dead at your feet an' knowin' yuh fixed him that way? I guess not. Yuh don't know a durned thing about sudden death!'

She moved around him. 'I still hate you!' she flashed. 'You're trying to twist things. It *was* your gun that killed Albert!'

'It's impossible to talk to yuh,' said Bill Corrigan. 'I've had my say. Just one thing, Miss—stick to your teaching

44

an' see if you can tell the kids how to figger out the difference between the truth an' lies.'

'You!' Her hand flew out to strike his face but he reacted with surprising speed. His arm went up. He caught her hand and held it for a moment before releasing her.

At that moment a voice said: 'Is this man bothering you, Miss?'

With the same swift response, Bill Corrigan turned and looked into the smiling face of the man he knew as Ed Hunter. Immaculately dressed, his black hat carefully brushed, his watch-chain glittering, he stood on the boardwalk, just behind the rancher.

'Yuh're stickin' your nose in, Cassidy man,' said Bill. 'This lady is not bein' bothered.'

'You hardly seem friendly.'

'We're not!'

Ed Hunter kept his hat in his hand, carefully pressed to his chest, as he turned to the girl. He was a model of deference. 'I know who you are, Miss Peek. You have taken a position at the school. Your brother is dead—a regrettable gun affair and you blame Mr Corrigan.'

Bill whistled. 'Yuh seem to know a lot.'

'I mention all this,' said Ed Hunter, 'because I may be able to help you, Miss Peek.'

'Help me? How?'

'I am very good at making inquiries,' he said softly. 'And I'm in a position to discover facts about your brother. I'll probably see you again and let you know the background to your brother's death.'

45

'Why should you do all this?' asked the girl.

'I just want to help—' began the man.

'You're workin' for the Cassidys,' Bill Corrigan ground out. 'What the hell are yuh gettin' at?'

'I work for the Cassidy brothers,' said Ed Hunter in his careful way, 'but don't let that throw you.'

And with that cryptic remark he almost bowed to the girl, replaced his hat and walked quickly away. Bill watched him narrowly and thought there was a lean, wiry spring to the man's step that was out of keeping with his deferential attitude.

'Now that jasper is a queer one,' said Bill, rubbing his chin.

The girl flashed him a look of scorn and then walked around him. He watched her go with a strange mixture of annoyance and a desire to make her understand his position. It was a useless thought, however, and he walked on.

His mind hardened back to one damnable fact; his ranch-house, over which he had slaved to build, was a charred ruin. He was not going to forget this body blow or the men who had done it. He walked back to the spot where he could see the Cassidy office and, thumbs in gunbelt, he stared.

Apparently in West Plains justice was going to be something you dealt out yourself. He thought that white-painted wood office building would burn quite easily.

46

Chapter Four

When the idea did occur he laughed at the simplicity of it. After all there are a few difficulties about setting fire to a building in broad daylight, in view of the general public, and arson was a word that had meaning even in a frontier town like West Plains. And he was damned if he'd do the dirty work at night or hire hellions to do it. The job would be done neatly right now and he was going to sit on the other side of the road and laugh like hell at the bonfire.

Bill Corrigan first went to a general store and bought a new fawn Stetson. He felt a sense of jauntiness with a new hat. He walked his horse to a livery and saw it made comfortable with a feed of oats. Then he bought an old ramshackle wagon from the same man and hired a steady old horse. He drove out and then called at another store and bought some cans of kerosene and some old sacks. He drove on, stopped in an alley and allowed the kerosene to leak over the sacks and the wagon. Then he hammered two spokes out of the right-hand side front wheel and wondered if the wheel would last for another hundred yards before collapsing.

He slipped the leathers on the harness so that he could unhitch the horse very quickly. Then, turning into the main stem again, he whipped the horse up to a gallop. The old wagon rattled and thumped crazily down the main street, causing two punchers to wheel their mounts, and then headed straight for the white-painted building that house the activities of the Cassidy brothers.

He had judged it neatly. The front wheel hit the porch of the building and, as he had hoped, collapsed. The wagon jarred into the frame of the office. Bill jumped down from his seat yelling: 'The wheel has collapsed!' A few sightseers paused to watch events. Not one of them saw the lick of flame near the wagon seat. Bill had left the sulphur matches burning as he had jumped down.

He yelled again to attract attention. 'The wheel has collapsed! Collapsed, durn it!'

All at once the sulphur matches reached the kerosene-soaked sacks and flames seared into the air. Whoosh!

'Durn it. The wagon's on fire!' he yelled at the top of his voice.

He slipped the horse out of the rig inside a minute. In that time the wagon was a torch that licked out to the other building.

He got the horse away and went across the road and hitched the animal to a tie-rail.

Flames shot yellowly to the porch roof and licked into the office walls. Men had already spilled from the building. The Cassidy brothers and their thin gunman were out there. Sep and Clark Cassidy were pleading with

48

strangers to do something and getting little response. The gunman, Hogan, was unmoved, and his black eyes had already picked out Bill Corrigan who was standing on the other side of the street, his arms folded and a grin on his face.

'What the hell's goin' on?' asked a man.

'Wheel collapsed an' the wagon caught fire,' said Bill promptly.

Another man asked the same question, and the answer was passed around. Bill Corrigan heard it repeated among the onlookers and he smiled grimly. And then Sheriff Dan Holladay came up and his barked inquiry was just the same.

'What's all this?'

'Wheel collapsed and the wagon fired!' said three voices.

The sheriff looked suspiciously at Bill Corrigan. 'You fixed this!'

'It was an accident.' Bill pointed at the blazing wagon. 'Take a look fast before it goes up in smoke—the front wheel collapsed.'

'That damned office is goin' up in smoke, too!' gritted the sheriff.

An attempt was made by public spirited citizens to get water buckets to the scene but there just was not enough organization and the effort was a failure.

Clark Cassidy pushed over to where Bill stood. 'You started this! Sheriff, arrest this man! This is deliberate!' His cold blue eyes sparked with unusual anger.

'You hear that, Corrigan?' the sheriff worried.

'I hear it and deny it. You ask the folks around here what happened. The wheel collapsed an' the wagon fired.'

'Why the devil should it fire?' Clark Cassidy snapped.

'Maybe a spark from the iron tyre.'

'What were you doing with kerosene?'

'Waal, now, I guess that's my business,' said Bill, 'but I don't mind answerin'. I need it on my ranch.'

'You think this is clever!' hissed Clark Cassidy. 'Well, you'll regret this trick!'

Bill Corrigan grabbed the man's collar and nearly lifted him off the ground. 'You're right, amigo—it isn't funny any longer! In fact, I'm plumb out of humour.' He dropped the other man again. Aware that another man was softly crowding him, he turned and stared into the white face of the gunman, Hogan.

'Maybe you want to start somethin',' Bill said quietly, and he glared a challenge into the other's eyes.

'There's a time an' place.' The man's reply was flat, as if devoid of interest.

'You could make it now!'

'I'll make it later.' It was the retort of an unemotional man who was not easily fooled. 'You'll die without fuss.'

'Then you'll die with me,' stated Corrigan coldly, and he turned to the old nag tied at the rail. Although the office was blazing and there was little likelihood of the conflagration being subdued, he had lost interest. Very probably this might just be a pin-prick in the hides of the Cassidy brothers. He led the horse away, back to the livery.

Burning the office had been a fool's play, he thought in dissatisfaction. It just did not solve anything. He wished for a just solution to a problem and the fire-raising was just a stunt which, on reflection, was not to his liking.

In an uneasy frame of mind, which the new Stetson did nothing to alleviate, he rode out of town. He intended to return to the ranch. As he rode, for some curious reason he began to think about the girl and the mental picture of those dark eyes and flushed cheeks actively hating him was something he wished would happen to another guy.

He began to wonder about himself. Sure, he had been forced into the gun-match with young Al Peek and he had had to fight for his life with the Irishman but if these events had not occurred he would have been happier. In fact, if he had met that girl in better circumstances—He broke off his thoughts, astounded at the trend!

'Damn!' he swore. 'Giddup, hoss! We're headin' for home—an' the hell with those Cassidy jaspers!'

When he rode into the ranch-yard and surveyed the charred place that was his home, the old grim feeling returned. There was a score to settle and by thunder he would not back down!

It was no use brooding. He sent the horse into the corral; went to the bunk-house. Bert Foggin met him.

51

'We've bin clearing up,' he cracked. 'Sam Hicks an' the other hand ha' gone out branding—me, I figured to have some chow an' start again on thet durned heap o' charcoal.'

'I'll give you a hand after I've eaten,' said Bill. 'Where the hell's Li Foo? Hope he's got some chow for me.'

He sat at a table in the bunk-house, rolled a cigarette while he waited for Li Foo to come up with the steak. The Chinaman appeared in due course, a tiny figure in shirt and denims much too large for him. His toothy smile greeted Bill Corrigan. Bare ankles in wood sandals clattered across the floor. 'Hi, Mister Colleegan—we got steak—you see!'

'I see. Let's have it—I'm hungry.'

He ate prime beef and onions and fried potatoes with the urgent satisfaction a big man with an appetite gets from good food. Eating was real—like breathing and sleeping.

He was not the sort of man to sit around while there was work to do, and a bit later he was helping Bert Foggin to clear away the charred sparring from the wrecked ranch-house. They worked steadily for two hours, dragging the rubbish to the rear of the ranch-yard, levelling the old site so that work could start again on a new building. Bill Corrigan was determined to erect another ranch-house which would be a replica of the old. Maybe he would add another wing, he reflected, wondering why the hell he needed another wing!

The site was clear, down to the foundation logs which

were untouched by the fire, so he left them in the ground.

'Right, we're ready to build,' he commented.

'Me—I figger the stars overhead an' a good bedroll is all a jigger needs!' cackled Bert Foggin.

'Yeah? You try that next January when the snows are here, old-timer.

'I done it,' said Bert promptly. 'Dug my way outa ten feet o' snow in Montana! Buried alive once! Rode through a durned blizzard fer four days once!'

'Sure—I know—you've done it all!' laughed Bill Corrigan.

They became aware of the rider moving slowly down the west trail, a man who sat his horse awkwardly as if riding a nag was a form of torture. They stared until the distant black slope on the plodding animal became a human being they could identify.

'It's Walt, from the Broken Horseshoe!' exclaimed Big Bill Corrigan.

'Never figgered he could sit a hoss!' rapped Bert.

It jarred into Corrigan's mind that the waiter must have some real news or an urgent need for twenty dollars because only that would persuade him to ride this distance.

Bill waited quietly for the man to ride up. He was certainly slow. As he came closer they saw his apparel was certainly old, for he wore a hat too big for him and a long jacket evidently cut for a man much larger. Eventually, he rode into the yard and halted his old black horse.

'I'd like a word with you, Mr Corrigan,' he muttered nervously.

'Yep. What brings yuh out, Walt?' asked Bill kindly.

The man leaned down from the horse, his face twitching. 'The twenty dollars . . . yuh promised . . . Mr Corrigan. . . .'

'You'll get it.' Bill leaned against the horse and stared expectantly at the man. Walt looked around as if the vast grasslands and hills had ears, and then his pale eyes fixed on Bert Foggin.

'I don't like talkin' in front of other guys,' he said.

'Bert is part of the fixtures,' sail Bill patiently. 'You got some new for me, Walt?'

'Aw right. Yeah, them two fellers that fired your ranch-house—I know them.'

'Names?' asked Bill grimly.

'One's called Blue Pete—big ranny—worked on the rail-road for some time. The other's his side-kick—a little jasper—jest know him as Nat.'

'Where do I find them?'

'They git in the Broken Horseshow most nights. Two dirty rannigans—they stink to hell—I figger they sleep in the barns—'

'Are yuh sure they are the men?' Bill pressed. 'How do yuh know?'

Walt tapped his forehead. 'I ain't silly, Mr Corrigan! I hear them talkin'—an' I can figger things out. They were plenty drunk last night.'

'Last night? Why didn't yuh tell me this earlier to-day?'

'I was scared, Mr Corrigan. I ain't brave. I thought some feller was watchin' me talk to yuh . . . them guys would smash me to bits if they knew . . . then I changed my mind. . . .'

'About talking to me? So you rode over. Did you make sure no one saw yuh ride up here?'

'I made sure,' said the other cunningly. 'I ain't a fool. An' you can take it from me it was Blue Pete and Nat that did this job. They was drunk an' boasting about a fire. I didn't figger it out at the time—but now I know. An' they had plenty o' dinero—not often they got the price o' more'n two drinks.'

'Yuh can stick around here for a few days if you're scared, Walt,' said Bill Corrigan quietly.

'I ain't scared too much now. Heh! Hey! Nobody's seen me ride out—an' they won't see me ride in! Got the money, Mr Corrigan?'

'I'll get it, Walt.' He strode off to the bunk-house. He had rescued the little strong-box last night along with his guns and clothes and papers, and he returned to the waiter with the promised twenty dollars. The man clutched the coins as if this was more than he had earned for some time.

They watched him ride out, a little faster this time, but still saddle-awkward.

They began again on the ranch-house site, measuring and squaring corners. There was a certain level of silence in the air, only the bellowing of some distant steers came to their ears. The vast valley and the surrounding hills trapped only noises that were natural to the land.

A few clouds sailed slowly, high in a blue sky that made a canopy over the endless earth. The sweetness of the spring air came as a tonic to the lungs of the men who worked in silence.

Then, ten minutes after Walt's slow horse had disappeared up the valley trail, they heard the sound of three distant gunshots. Corrigan and Bert Foggin straightened and stared, waiting for another sound, as if it might provide an answer to unspoken questions.

But the land wore its normal atmosphere of peace and quiet like the gloved hand of a lady.

But two men knew there was something amiss.

'Git the horses!' snapped Corrigan. 'Let's ride out!'

They rode down the trail with a thunder of hoofs on the hard earth, creating a plume of dust to mark their ride. They careered around the base of green hills, startled some wandering steers in a grassy coulee with their rapid approach. They flattened low against the horses's necks, nostrils picking up the sudden animalish sweat. Skirting a glade of larch and cedar, they rounded a fold in the land. Bill Corrigan saw, with sickening finality, the thing that had happened.

Walt's horse was cropping grass under a tree. Ten yards away, in the tall grass and wild-flowers, lay the black shape of a man.

Corrigan threw himself off his horse as he came up. One glance was enough. Blood made a horrible pool near the man. It trickled down his cheek from a hole in the head, and it seeped from another ugly patch on his shirt near his heart. There was a third bullet wound, low in the waist, which added to the ghastly odour of a butcher's shop.

Walt was dead. He had been ambushed at close quarters, shot down, evidently, without a chance.

It seemed the nervous old waiter from the Broken Horseshoe had not been careful enough in riding out of town. Or maybe he had just rode into some lurking gunmen who knew too much.

Obviously there had been some motive behind this killing. Walt was a nonentity. He had no friends and he had no enemies. He had been slaughtered for one reason only and Corrigan knew what it was.

He straightened; stared around at the silent land. He would find the killer. Maybe he would kill his third man in West Plains before long. He was being forced into dicing with death by events he did not seek.

'Poor devil!' he muttered. 'Cut down—buffaloed! Now who was it?'

Old Bert Foggin was rubbing his whiskers and making unpleasant noises in his throat. 'Durn it, they shouldn't ha' done that! Walt was nuthin' to nobody!'

'I'm to blame,' said Bill grimly. 'Let's mosey around. Could be we'll find some tracks.'

'Too many danged steers been thisaway for that,' grunted Bert.

'We'll look,' stated Corrigan. 'See, there's been a hoss here with new shoes! Let's look at Walt's black.'

'Thet old nag ain't got new irons, I'll guess,' returned Bert.

Examination of the animal proved he was right and

they began to track around. They took the black horse in town. In some soft soil, near an underground spring, they picked up the distinctive hoof-marks again.

'A new set of shoes,' stated Bill Corrigan.

'Yuh aimin' to look at every hoss in the territory that's been shoed lately?' asked Bert.

'Nope. I'm just lookin', pardner—an' if you'd quit chin-wagging so much yuh might discover somethin'!'

'I wus trackin' with Indians afore yuh was born!' boasted the oldster. 'Old Big Eye—he wus chief of a Cheyenne lodge—said to me—'

'For the love of Pete, don't give me that old yarn again!' interrupted Corrigan.

He rode away to an indignant stare from Bert. Except for some indistinct muttering from the old man, they cast around in silence for further sign but it was an almost impossible task on the hard grassland. Bill Corrigan had to give up. He reined in; looked at Bert.

'I've got a job for yuh. Ride into West Plains an' get the undertaker to come out here with a four-wheel rig and a coffin.'

'I c'd jest ride old Walt in over his hoss.'

'And have him thrown in a hole in boothill!' snarled Corrigan. 'Yuh git into town like I said. Walt is having a proper burial. You can hit the trail now, oldster.'

'Guess you're the boss,' grunted Bert. He added: 'An' it's your dinero yuh're wastin'!'

Corrigan took the body back to the bunk-house, cleaned blood from the man's face. There was nothing more he could do. He washed his own hands. It was

58

quiet around the spread except for the sound of the horses in the corral circling the fence. He almost wished Sam Hicks or the other hand would appear. Restlessly, he went back to his horse and rode out, swinging the yard gate behind him, making the sign-board above swing. Double C. He had painted it himself; maybe it needed freshening.

It was damned hard to explain, but he had a fool hunch that somewhere out in the rolling grasslands was a hellion who had gunned down poor old Walt.

He rode out, in a new direction, like a man will start an almost aimless search for something, somewhere, hoping but hardly knowing where he will find what he seeks.

He circled a grassy mound quite close to the ranch-yard; halted the mustang immediately he heard the solitary sound.

Somewhere an unseen man had coughed.

The hillock rose sweet with grama grass and purple flowers, land fit for all the cattle and horses a man might possess. It was also handy for a man who wanted to hide.

Bill Corrigan slipped from the horse and walked along the base of the mound. His boots just slipped noiselessly through the long grass. His gun slid into his hand.

He saw the man sitting astride his horse. He was rolling a cigarette with slow, casual fingers as if he had plenty of time. He was a black shadow against the greenness—black shirt, hat and pants. An ominous man.

It was Hogan, the Cassidy brothers's hired gunny.

Chapter Five

Bill Corrigan spent two very long minutes observing the gunman and in that time he came to some conclusions.

The man was waiting for someone. Who the someone might be was a bit of a mystery. And the reason for the meeting was also strange.

Yet the gunman was out here only a stone's throw from the Double C. Was he seeking a gun show-down? And was this the man who had killed Walt?

If he could examine the shoes of the man's horse, he might get an answer to that last query.

He could call the man down now, reach for guns and get it over with. One of them would undoubtedly be dead.

All the same he would like to discover why the man was waiting. He would like to see the other person if, in fact, this was a rendezvous.

Bill Corrigan slipped quietly away, back to his horse. The gun-play could come later.

He rode a wide loop back to the ranch-yard, saw Li Foo scurrying in and out of the bunk-house. Corrigan ran his horse into the corral and left it saddled. He checked his Colt, spun the chambers and then returned it to the holster. He walked out of the yard and across to the barn, a big clapboard building he had built himself. There was a hay-loft in the barn which he could reach by a long ladder from the ground. There were no windows in the barn; just a single hatchway under the roof through which hay could be hauled for storage by means of a hook and rope.

From this open hatch a good view of the grassy mound could be obtained. He could not actually see Hogan, but the moment the man moved out he would be under observation. And if he met up with someone there would be time to digest the facts.

Corrigan waited.

He had not forgotten old Walt. The presence of Hogan was suspicious but it was not proof that he had gunned the old waiter down. That proof might come later. And if it was proved, it was plain murder, for Walt did not carry a gun and could not have defended himself.

Corrigan waited a long time for some movement from behind the grassy mound. As the time passed, he wondered if Hogan had moved on, down the valley, but as that just did not add up he knew the man was still there, waiting.

At long last the period of ominous patience was over as he saw a glimpse of dark broadcloth against the grass. Then Hogan rode out, tall in the saddle and dark as the night.

One—two—three seconds elapsed and then another rider moved slowly into view behind him.

It was the girl, Miss Peek—the sister of the man he had been forced to kill!

A cold anger against this girl settled inside Bill Corrigan's guts like a fog on a hillside. This seemed unbelievable. That she should ally herself with this gunman was an outrage against commonsense. He was ready to believe that her judgement was distorted because of her grief over her brother—and that was misplaced because he had not been much good by all accounts—but to side with a hired gunny must be utterly unnatural in a girl—a school marm, at that.

Why they had arranged to meet, he did not know. She could have rode out with the man in the first instance.

As far as Hogan was concerned, there could only be one reason for his presence on the Double C.

He was seeking a gun-fight, confident in his proved skill with two Colts.

He stared grimly. The girl was clad in riding kit, dark jeans, a blue blouse or shirt and a fawn hat. Seeing her dressed like this, she seemed more like a lithe boy than the very feminine woman he had met earlier.

The two riders picked a way slowly towards the ranch-yard. Hogan sat his horse with easy skill, a man of the trails. The girl lagged behind. They reached the pole fence and Hogan waited for the girl, turning in the saddle. Corrigan watched them exchange a few words and, with narrowed eyes, he wondered what had been said.

Incredulously, he wondered why the girl was here at all. Hogan he could understand; the man had been sent to do a job by his bosses. Hogan would do it, like shooting the head off a rattler. There was nothing in this man's motivations to wonder about.

The two riders opened the pole gate and the horses crow-hopped into the yard.

With hard pupils in slitted eyes, Corrigan saw Li Foo stand on the bunk-house steps and make chattering noises in Cantonese. A shout came from Hogan.

'Corrigan!'

It was a drawled yell, like a command, almost derisi-sive. The man got down from his horse and walked away from it and then halted. His thin body threw a menace that was not physical because he packed little muscle, and yet this black-clothed man looked evil.

His next shout contained a hint of impatience. 'Corrigan!'

Bill stood in the open space of the hatch and stared down. He made no answer and did not reveal his presence by a single sound. He waited.

He figured the man could fry a little. It might be bad for his nerves—if he had any. It would be better if he moved in closer—the range would be improved. And a man shooting downwards at a target has an advantage. The gun is a split second ahead, when leaving leather, of a gun having to shoot at an upward angle.

'Corrigan!' There was no anger in the shout. 'I know you're here.'

Bill glanced at the girl as she sat her horse, motionless,

by the yard rails. Her face seemed set, shaded by her hat, and almost inscrutable. He wondered fleetingly about her motives in meeting up with this gunman. Right at that moment he did not understand the girl.

He thought he had made Hogan wait long enough. The man's head turned slowly, scrutinizing the ranch buildings, but always returned to look at the bunkhouse. Clearly, he considered Bill Corrigan was inside the building.

'Hogan!' The call drifted across the ranch-yard, a gentle reminder of reality. Bill had not shouted the name.

The gunman's head whipped and then froze on the man standing high in the open hatchway.

'You want me, Hogan?' Bill mocked.

The thin man nodded almost imperceptively. He did not move and his hands were hovering above the twin guns. He seemed to be assessing the situation.

'I'm here,' said Bill Corrigan easily. Perhaps he could taunt this man out of his professional icy calmness. 'I see yuh've brought a lady with you! What's the idea?'

Hogan did not answer. He simply maintained his direct stare. However, the girl was provoked into a reply.

'I want to see you die!' she suddenly screamed.

'Still after revenge!' Corrigan commented. 'Well! Well!'

'I'm a witness!' she screamed again. The pitch of her voice testified to her taut nerves. She was close to hysteria.

'A witness!' repeated Corrigan. 'Why? D'yuh want to see sudden death? Is it a game?'

'I'll testify that this is a fair fight!' she shouted. 'That's why I arranged to meet Mr Hogan.'

'Fair fight, huh! Waal, that's more than old Walt got.' Corrigan's lips drawled the words while his narrowed eyes watched Hogan's hands.

'What do you mean?' She stared up at this tall man framed in the barn hatchway.

'Old Walt, the waiter from the Broken Horseshoe, was gunned down only a mile from here,' said Bill coldly. 'And I figger your gunny friend killed him. Plain murder. It would seem he guessed why Walt rode out here—to give me information.'

The girl had to control her restless horse. Then she gasped: 'You're trying to rile me! I don't know anything about old Walt!'

'Yuh do now,' snapped Bill.

'I don't want to know! You killed my brother! I'm going to be a witness that this is a fair fight! I will—'

'Yuh're bein' used,' said Bill brutally. 'By the Cassidys! No one cares about yuh bein' a witness except the Cassidy boys! What kept yuh, anyway? I saw Hogan here a long time ago!' He was taunting them, saying anything and watching the sombre twin guns.

'I had to stay with my class!' she flashed.

'Sure, sure! The school marm who likes death!'

'I hate you!'

Her horse jigged nervously and she edged it through

65

c

the yard gate. All the time she screamed: 'You deserve to die! You killed my brother!'

She was slightly crazy with hate and fear and distorted motives. Also, now that the time had arrived for the terrible showdown, she was unsure and afraid. The whole horrible mixup reflected in her voice.

'Okay!' bawled Corrigan. 'When yuh git back to town, tell the sheriff who killed old Walt, will yuh?'

'Corrigan!' It was Hogan's voice, with a trace of anger.

'Yeah?'

'Yuh've yapped long enough,' said the man.

Corrigan sensed rather than observed the swift downward claw for the twin guns and he was not a fraction of a second late in response. His hand whipped for the gun butt. A second of living seemed to hold an eternity and then his solitary Colt was blasting, mingling with the other shots. It was probably the fastest draw of his life. In that same fateful second of gun-clawing and blasting lead, he felt a sudden agony of pain and blackness rushed through his brain and drowned all thought and observation.

He fell into the dark trough that was neither life nor death and swam sickeningly down to the depths. He lay there for a long time, in the darkness, a barely breathing, almost non-living entity. The black void held him and cradled him and time had no meaning. Then there was pain but there was no relationship with his physical body. The pain was all of him and not tied to movement, for he could not move.

Bill Corrigan hovered between life and death and was aware of neither time nor place. A Colt slug had cut a track to the bone along the right side of his head, and another bit of lead had lodged near his heart.

The products of two guns that had fired with almost complete accuracy. Almost.

For a long time the proximity to near death held, and the world beyond his consciousness was a jumble of distant voices and dim faces that danced close to him and peered at him. Slowly, these vision clarified as strength returned. His sight improved and just to open his eyes did not result in a sickening swirl of sense and proportion. One day he realized he had moved an arm without pain racking through his flesh. The faces that peered at him became vaguely familiar although he did not comprehend that these were people he should know. Voices addressing him added to the unreality, causing confusion and protesting pains in his head.

Then there were periods of rest when nothing or no one intruded, and when the faces and voices moved in again he was considerably stronger. Understanding came slowly. One day he recognized a face.

'Bert Foggin!' he whispered feebly.

The answering rush of words caused him to shut his eyes and he did not understand any part of it.

But another day dawned and there were people at his bed again. A man stared grimly. The dark hair and dark eyes of a girl looked straight at him.

'Sam—Hicks—' he muttered. 'Where—am—I?' He looked again. 'You! But—I don't get it—'

'I'm Sylvia Peek,' she said. 'Don't you recognize me?'
'I—I—'

'He's just gettin' to figger things out,' muttered Sam Hicks. 'Don't rush him.'

She had waited a long time to say the things in her mind and words tumbled out in an intensity of emotions.

'I—I'm so sorry—for everything—you nearly died! I'm a fool! I didn't understand! Oh, I want so much to apologize! Perhaps when you're well—'

'He'll be okay,' said Sam's voice. 'An't don't yuh git upset, miss. Yuh've nursed this feller for weeks!'

'I had to! I had to! Oh, what a fool I was!'

'He's got a long way to go afore he's strong again,' said Sam Hicks. 'An' when he's well again there'll be a big score to settle.'

'They'll have him killed,' said the girl helplessly. 'What can we do?'

'Keep him hidden out here where they can't find him.'

'Yes, we must keep him hidden.'

To Bill Corrigan there seemed to be a screen between him and the torrent of words. He felt a stirring of desire to understand and reply but his mind and lips would not respond. Even to attempt to cross the chasm was an effort and he closed his eyes and faded back into the comfortable land of non-existence.

A day later they were there again, talking, trying to arouse his awareness. He answered once or twice, vaguely. He was in bed, he knew, and that made sense.

The room was a cabin somewhere, with log walls and clay-packed joints. An Indian blanket kept him warm.

Another day followed and this time a gleam came to Corrigan's eyes as he recognized old Bert Foggin again.

'Hi, Bert!'

'Say, yuh're looking almost whole agin!' The whiskery visage grinned. 'Almost as tough as me, amigo!'

'Am—I—tough—Bert,' he muttered. He looked to the left of the bed. The girl was there, her dark eyes wide and anxious. 'Yuh here—again,' he said.

'She's bin here all the time,' chirped Bert Foggin. 'Waal, most o' the times—me an' Sam Hicks done took turns.'

'Where am I?' His eyes flickered with sudden mental energy.

'It's a line cabin high in the hills.'

'Why?' he lipped.

'We took yuh to Doc Lawson when we figured yuh was dead,' said Bert Foggin. 'Took yuh out o' that barn with this gal cryin' over yuh. Thet galoot Hogan had gotten to his hoss and rode away—leavin' blood all over the gosh-darned place. Yuh plugged him right enough —you followin' me, boss?'

'So far—yes' said Corrigan tiredly.

'Waal, yuh were at Doc Lawson's place only one night when some jasper tried to git in the window an' finish you off. Sam Hicks was there an' went for his gun. Don't rightly know iffen he hit this feller—maybe he didn't. Anyway another galoot tried the same trick two nights later. We figured to move yuh even though Doc Lawson said any movement might kill yuh.'

'So? Why didn't yuh take me back to the ranch an' the bunk-house?' It was a long speech and Bill felt weary but his brain was working, seizing on the salient points and he wanted to know.

Bert Foggin seemed to glance at the girl. Then: 'I don't reckon yuh should oughta bother yourself any-more today about this an' that, boss.'

'I want to know.' Fiercely.

'Waal – they fired the barn an' the bunk-house. Them Cassidy brothers ha' got gunmen everywhere. Must be paying pretty high for these hellions—and they got other rascals runnin' off Double C. stock every night. Me an' Sam Hicks jest can't keep track o' the rustling—but afore long there won't be a danged steer left on Double C.'

It was a hard blow to aim at a sick man and only an oldster like Bert Foggin, accustomed to the cruelty of the west, would have dealt it. Corrigan took it in silence as if nursing his strength to deal with the facts.

'Anything else?' he asked in a whisper.

'The Cassidy brothers don't know where yuh are,' said Bert. 'We've bin dodgin' around like hell to shake 'em off everytime we ride up to this shack.'

'Bert, that's enough for one day!' exclaimed Sylvia Peek.

'Heck, he kin take it,' boasted the oldster. 'The harder yuh hit the tougher this man gits! Yessir, them Cassidy men want you dead, boss. Best thing yuh can do is get well, boss, an' buckle on two guns. I'll ride all the way with yuh!'

In his rough old way Bert was displaying the brand of loyalty that kept men together on almost forlorn hopes.

'And Hogan?' whispered Corrigan.

'Still alive, I guess. Naturally, I ain't met up with that gink or maybe we'd have bin reachin' for hoglegs— but he's still around and I reckon he'd like to clear leather again when he sees you.'

Corrigan nodded imperceptibly. 'All right, Bert. Thanks for—everything—' He suddenly felt tired again and the warmth of the bed defeated him temporarily.

'He's got to rest,' said Sylvia Peek.

'Sure—waal, I reckon what I said will put him on his feet in a day or so!'

Bert Foggin walked to a window and looked out, wariness now a habit. Sylvia Peek glanced down at Corrigan, saw that his eyes were closed.

She placed a hand to her lips and then lightly touched his cheek with the transferred kiss.

She stared at the long scar on the right side of his head, where the black and grey hair would never grow again, and then she got up and approached old Bert.

'There's a rider comin',' said the oldster. 'It's him again. Now I can't figger that guy out! What's he want this time—unless it's jest to see yuh, miss?'

She stared through the broken glass. 'Ed Hunter! Again! I wish he'd leave me alone! Still, I'll say this— he hasn't given us away to the Cassidy brothers—as yet!'

71

Chapter Six

They met him at the door, with Bert Foggin lightly touching his gun in his holster, his old eyes bright with speculation. 'Yeah? What d'yuh want, Mister Hunter?'

'How is the patient?' asked the man mildly.

'Better'n the last time yuh was here.'

'Good.' He fingered his watch chain. He held his hat in courteous deference and looked at the girl. 'And you, Sylvia, you must be tired—working at the school and riding up here almost daily.'

'I'm all right. I must do what I can for him.'

'Of course. But I'm worried about you.'

'Why? Do the Cassidys know about this place?' she asked.

'No. Otherwise they would have sent Hogan up here with his gun.' His handsome face was grave. 'You're running a risk, Sylvia, because they are determined to eliminate Corrigan. I hate to see you running that risk.'

'You're employed by Sep and Clark Cassidy!' she flashed.

'Only as an office manager—a business advisor.'

'I wonder what they are planning now!' she said bitterly. 'Those two greedy men are trying to take over the town. Oh, what a fool I was not to see the truth earlier!'

'There have been men like them before in western towns,' he said quietly. 'And they don't always last. They prosper as long as the law is weak. Sep and Clark Cassidy are only succeeding because there seems no one strong enough to stand against them.'

'Corrigan was strong,' she said bitterly. 'But now they are destroying him. I must have been mad—out of my mind—to seek revenge in his death. I knew that the moment the guns crashed through the air and—he—he fell—'

'Well, nothing is solved,' said Ed Hunter. 'The Cassidy brothers are busy breaking Tom Selby. They are taking over his lumber business—I have been preparing papers. They have strong-arm men out at the lumber camp.' He paused. 'They have something on Tom Selby that I don't understand—'

'We don't understand you!' she flashed.

'You will some day,' he murmured.

'Why do you profess friendship for us and at the same time side with the Cassidys?'

'I just work for them.'

'Then you are actively trying to destroy Tom Selby—and Bill Corrigan!'

'Not really. I could reveal the whereabouts of this cabin to Sep Cassidy—but I will not.' He smiled. 'If I didn't have this job, some other man would—and he might be harder than me.' He added hurriedly: 'I can't tell you any more.'

'Yuh ain't tellin' us anything, Mister Hunter!' snapped old Bert Foggin. 'Jest that you work for them snakeroos!'

'Don't let it throw you, Bert,' said the other with a sudden hard, mocking timbre in his voice.

Bert's whiskery jaw thrust out. 'I'm a tough hombre to throw—'

'Sure, sure! Well, I thought I'd ride up to see Miss Peek—I'm concerned about her safety.'

'Oh, I'm all right, Mr Hunter—thank you.'

There was a gleam of admiration in his eyes that enabled the girl, with the intuition of her sex, to read his mind. So he was susceptible! Well, he was a handsome man, always immaculate and clean, although possibly a little older than Bill Corrigan—at least in his mid-thirties. She broke off her thoughts helplessly. What on earth was she thinking about!

'Mr Hunter!' The call came strongly from the bed in the centre of the cabin. 'What do yuh want up here?'

Ed Hunter moved forward and smiled down at Corrigan.

'I've been here before, when you were unconscious. I'm concerned for Sylvia's safety—and yours. I thought I'd ride up, look around for strangers on the trail and give you some news.'

'What news? Yuh figure to tell me the Cassidys are out to ruin me—burn my ranch and run off my cattle?'

'You know that? Well, it's true and I can't stop them.'

'Why should yuh stop them?' asked Bill harshly.

'Yuh get your bread an' butter from them! Yuh're a Cassidy man!'

Ed Hunter's jaw tightened and he slapped one fist into the palm of his other hand. 'I draw wages, Corrigan. Sure. I also know more about the Cassidy brothers's business affairs than any other man in West Plains and pretty soon that will be important.'

'What sort o' game are you playing, man?'

The smile returned to Ed Hunter's face. 'The world is full of people, Corrigan—the hunters and the hunted —eat or be eaten—'

'What's that supposed to mean?' Bill's voice rasped with new-found anger.

'You will learn some day,' said the other. 'In the meantime you should be interested to know that Tom Selby is being run off his own property, your ranch is being systematically plundered, a new saloon has been opened in the town, owned by the Cassidys, where no-limit gambling will soon have half the town in debt to Sep and Clark Cassidy.'

'Gambling has been strictly controlled in West Plains.' Corrigan tried to sit up and the girl put out a detaining hand.

'Not any longer. Sheriff Holladay is weak.' Ed Hunter paused. 'Before long he will be taking bribes. I know the pattern—but maybe I'll get documentary proof—' He broke off.

'I'm getting' up!' muttered Corrigan, and he moved the bedclothes.

'You've got to rest,' cried the girl. 'You're still weak!'

'Lie in bed, huh, while those two sneakin' coyotes smash me—rustle my stock!'

He swung his legs over the bedside and the whole world swirled in a sickening black-out. He did not know it but he toppled slowly sideways and his eyes closed like those of a child going to sleep.

'Keep him in bed,' said Ed Hunter. 'If you're riding back now, Sylvia, I'll go with you.'

'Yuh do that, Mister,' yapped Bert Foggin. 'I'll stick around here. Sam Hicks is out tryin' to keep track of what is goin' on down at the Double C. Yuh watch out now! Iffen thet Hogan galoot got on your tail you'd shore be in trouble—yuh bein' without a hogleg, Mister Hunter! Heh! Heh!'

The man in the immaculate store suit smiled carefully as he escorted the girl outside to the waiting horses.

Two nights of restless malaise brought crazy dreams to Bill Corrigan in which Sep Cassidy's evil face smiled down at him and Hogan drew guns endlessly. The man's black shape swirled in a grey cloud and then resolved into Sylvia Peek's dark beauty and then faded as bawling cattle stampeded through his nightmare. He was stronger through the day and aware that Sam Hicks tended him one day and then Bert Foggin the next. Only the night nurtured the wild mental images and at the base of this orgy of thoughts grew a sullen desire for revenge.

On the second day after Ed Hunter's visit he carefully placed his legs out of the bed and tested the feel of the hard-baked earth floor under his feet. He felt surprisingly strong. His head was fine and his brain clear as a bell. He stood up. He grinned at Bert Foggin and ran a hand over his growth of beard.

'I'm nearly as whiskery as you! Git me my pants an' shirt. An' git a long-handled razor.'

'You shore yuh feel all right?'

'Yep. I've got work to do. Where's my gun! An' find me a Winchester an' shells. Yuh got my horse any-wheres around here?'

'Told thet gal you'd be stompin' around in a few days!' said Bert, delighted. 'Shore got your horse! Shore got everythin'!'

'Where is Sylvia?' asked Bill slowly.

'Ain't bin back since she rode away wi' that Ed Hunter feller.'

'Is that so?' He buckled on his gunbelt, looked at the Colt that had nearly taken Hogan. The gun was oiled and working fine. It seemed that Bert or Sam Hicks had not taken a depressed view of his future.

'I'll rustle some grub while you're fixin' tuh make yourself pretty!' snapped Bert. 'You got to eat. Doc Lawson said that—an' he ought to know.'

'Does he know I'm here?' Bill jerked a thumb around the cabin.

'Nope. He jest knows we took youh away from his place.'

'Yuh been to see him again?'

'Sure. We had to git some medicene.'

'How many people know I'm here?'

'Jest me an' Sam—an' thet gal an' Ed Hunter.'

'Where's Sam now?'

'Why he's probably moseyin' around the Double C. Its kinda tricky around there on account yuh never know when yuh will ride into gun-totin' strangers.'

Bill Corrigan stretched to his full height and walked around the cabin. He wondered grimly how his body would react if he had to move fast. Had he the strength to thrust back into a fight with the Cassidy brothers and their hired badmen? He thought he would find out— the hard way.

'Did the sheriff do anythin' about old Walt's killing?' he asked as he got ready to shave.

'Nary a thing—'crept yap about proof. I got the poor galoot decently buried.' Bert stoked the round iron stove in the middle of the cabin.

'It's a waste o' time to wonder if he ever got around to investigating why my ranch buildings were fired,' said Corrigan. 'But I'm going to rouse that no-good badge-toter. I'm sending for the U.S. Marshal at Laramie. I reckon we need a new sheriff in West Plains for a start.'

'Say, why don't yuh jest go gunnin' for them Cassidys?' asked Bert eagerly.

'Yuh old coyote, there is law and order even in these territories—an' I'm not the law! Now quit yappin' an' get that grub set up. I'm hungry!'

'It's comin' up, boss.'

'And what happened to Li Foo?'

'I guess he jest run off. Ain't seen hair or hide o' him.' Bert had bacon sizzling in a pan.

'And the other hand?'

'He moseyed, too. Didn't like Colt fire, I guess.'

'Hmm.' Bill Corrigan tested the razor. 'Seems like I owe you and the others some time by now. Guess I'll have to git the money from the Union Bank when I ride into town.'

'An' shoot them jaspers up?' asked Bert eagerly.

'Are you loco? This isn't an owl-hoot town. I've told yuh—I'll get the Marshal from Laramie—maybe some one witnessed the burning of my ranch buildings. Maybe I'll make those two hellions talk—the fellers Walt told me about—Blue Pete and his side-kick—what was it— Nat!'

'Maybe,' growled Bert and he rattled the pan on the stove. 'Talk, huh? That why yuh're fixin' that Colt .45 and totin' that Winchester for your saddle?'

'I need them,' said Bill Corrigan, 'for when I talk to Hogan!'

There was grim purpose about him a bit later when he stepped out of the cabin and looked around at the warm, fresh morning. A new sense of vigour held him and he wondered if it would last. He was washed, shaved, clothed in a new checked shirt and flapping vest. Sam Hicks had brought the gear to the cabin a few days back. Corrigan's familiar riding boots and pants were still good. His blood-soaked shirt had long ago been discarded. He had a new hat and it was okay except where it sat the still tender scar along his temple. His big legs felt strong as he walked to the hitched horse behind the cabin, carrying the Winchester. He checked the leathers on the horse, noted the animal was fat

79

through its enforced easy spell. Bert came up to him, carrying a saddle-bag for his mustang.

'Sure yuh feel all right, boss?'

'Good enough. I'll be better when I ride.'

'Sure. Maybe we'll meet up wi' Sam—or that gal.'

The girl. Sylvia. Corrigan paused while conjectures flooded his mind. She had stopped hating him. She had glimpsed the truth concerning him and her brother. She had nursed him to health, probably washed his face and changed his bandages with a woman's instinctive care for the unfortunate.

His mouth twisted grimly. Maybe she had helped him a great deal, but he could not remember much of that. What had stuck in his mind, during the raving nights of near delirium, was a picture of that dark-eyed beauty close to the black shape of the gunman, screaming: 'I want to see you die!'

How often in his distorted dreams, while pain stabbed from his skull wound, he had remembered her passionate cry: 'I hate you!'

'Yeah, the girl,' muttered Corrigan. 'She sided with Hogan again me.'

He wished he could forget that.

The line cabin was concealed in an inaccessible fold of the hills, about ten miles from the Double C ranch-yard. It was open range and just a few miles out of his boundaries. Once this remote cabin had been part of another ranch but when the owner had died new boundaries had been drawn. The cabin was a good hide-out and had served a purpose. Now it was time to leave.

West Plains was about seven miles away down another trail.

They rode easily, Corrigan silent and old Bert yapping like an old woman. When they finally stopped to view the charred remains of the Double C buildings, Corrigan felt a hard lump of pure hatred rise in his throat.

His home—his total ambition! The careful work of bare hands, hours of toil, the driving desire to create something that was his very own—now a gaunt pile of charred timbers rooted in a soil of black ash. He swung an angry face to the grassy hills all around. So far as he could see there was no sign of stock. No distant sound betrayed a wandering herd; only the wind sighing through the cottonwoods was a reminder of the old Double C.

He fingered the red, tender scar along his temple; felt it throb with his inward anger. Men had done this to him. Ruthless, avaricious men, known and unknown, the bosses and the hirelings. If he didn't seek revenge and justice, he wasn't a man!

He wheeled his horse. 'Let's go,' he said tersely.

'Where now, boss?'

'West Plains. I've seen all I want to see.'

'What you figgering on?'

'Two men,' said Bill Corrigan. 'They seem handy with a tar torch—this Blue Pete an' Nat. Maybe there's others like to fire a man's property. Then there's a gunny called Hogan—two guns, by thunder! Still it only needs one slug! Then we've got Sep an' Clark

81

Cassidy—two skunks in the background, money-men, killer hirers.'

'Them two!' exclaimed Bert in disgust. 'Don't even pack a gun! Don't even ride a hoss if they kin help it! Seems they jest sit around an' write sums on bits o' paper! Skunks—yuh're right there, boss!'

Corrigan nodded, patted the horse's neck, stared across the horizon in the direction of West Plains and knew that to ride there meant using a gun.

He was riding.

Two miles out of the town they met up with Sam Hicks. He was alone, riding a spirited little mustang, one of the Double C. remuda. His big honest face cracked in a grin when he saw Corrigan. 'Yuh're in the saddle!'

'There's work to do, Sam.'

'Yep. I've been in town. Drove some prime two-year-olds to the stockyards an' sold them at a good price. I put the money into the Union Bank an' Mr Cross is seein' to it. Yuh need dinero iffen yuh want to build them ranch-house an' barns again. An' I figured better to sell than allow them cattle to git rustled.'

Corrigan nodded. 'Good. Let's ride back to town. I want a telegraph message sent to Laramie requesting the U.S. Marshal to come here an' investigate the sheriff's office, for a start. I'd like to find out which lousy cattle buyer is payin' for rustled stock. Maybe somebody will talk. Some crooked waddies must ha' drove that cattle.'

They entered the bustling town, three men on whom silence suddenly descended. Even Bert quit moving his jaws. The town took them into its busy arms and they seemed to lose identity, mingling with the people, punchers taking time off, freight drivers, a blacksmith talking to a barber, women visiting shops, children playing in a school yard and hens scratting in the dust behind Mulligan's Store.

Corrigan went to the telegraph office and got the operator to send the message. Grimly, he came out. That was one chore completed but a week might elapse before the Marshal showed up. He rode with his two men to the timber yard and placed an order for clapboard and twelve-by-six posts, to be delivered to the ranch yard in two days. Another start. He then visited the Union Bank and, after a talk, found he still had money in the bank and his credit was good. After that he and Sam Hicks went to the sheriff's office while Bert Foggin took spritely steps into the Broken Horseshoe Saloon.

Corrigan stared at Dan Holladay. 'Yuh might as well know—I've sent for the U.S. Marshal from Laramie.'

'You've no authority—' the other began and got to his feet, indignation twisting his mouth and moustache.

'Any citizen has the right!' snapped Corrigan. 'And another thing—how much durned investigating have yuh done regarding the burning of my ranch buildings?'

'Now I'm lookin' into that, Corrigan,' spluttered the sheriff. 'Yessir!'

'I've had stock rustled.'

'I don't know anythin' about that.'

'Yuh know now. And Walt, the waiter at the Broken Horseshoe, was murdered an' I figure it was Hogan, the

Cassidy hired gunman. Have yuh questioned him?'

'Now you look here, Corrigan—'

Anger spilled out of Bill Corrigan. He grabbed the other man by his shirt. 'Yuh're just plain scared o' trouble, isn't that right? Waal, yuh'd better git started on somethin' or hand that badge in.'

'I'm the sheriff around here!' said Holladay shrilly. 'An'—an'—take your hands off me or I'll throw yuh in the hoosegow!'

'Jest button up!' gritted Corrigan and he turned and went outside.

The scar on his temple throbbed again. He said to Sam Hicks. 'That fool is nothing but a durned office clerk! How the hell he got elected, I don't know.'

They tramped to the Broken Horseshoe, leading the horses, pausing only to stare at the new saloon just across the road. One or two men went in and out of the bat-wings. There was the sound of a tinkling piano.

Old Bert Foggin had a bottle and a glass in front of him at a pine table and he was talking to an unshaven rannigan in bucksins. He looked up. 'Hyar, boss. Say, I hope yuh got a dollar for this hooch! Now this feller knows thet Blue Pete an' his little side-kick, Nat.'

Corrigan leaned forward. 'Where are they? I've been told they sneak in here when they've got some money.'

'Won't be around here fer a few days,' said the man. 'I heerd they're doin' some work up in the forest fer thet lumber camp an' that seems mighty queer to me 'cause —heh! Heh!' The man laughed. 'They weren't rightly particular about work!'

84

'Tom Selby's place!' Corrigan straightened. 'Waal, he wouldn't hire those two workshy drifters. That means the Cassidy brothers placed those two up there.'

'Say, boss, yuh want a drink?'

'Some other time, Bert. Now you just keep out o' trouble, old-timer. Sam and me are riding up to Tom Selby's place.'

'Yuh aim to start shootin'? 'Cause if yuh are, I'm a-going!'

'I want yuh to stick around here. Keep a look out, amigo. Maybe you'll hear somethin' about rustled beef. And maybe you can keep an eye on any movement of the Cassidys. Or that durned sheriff.'

They left the protesting oldster to the consolation of his bottle and rode out of the town. They put the horses to a canter on the open trail, easing them off as they headed into the hills. Timber began to show up in clumps with the inevitable juniper thickets. This became thicker and after two hours hard ride the forest of pine and cedar stretched before them. Two lumbering mule-drawn wagons came down the deeply rutted track, laden with sawn logs. The mule skinners were singing raucously on the down gradient, some old obscene song of the lumber camps.

When Corrigan and Sam Hicks rode into the main camp they noticed the gunman standing at Tom Selby's office door. He was a small man, young, with a confident, arrogant manner. He stuck his thumbs in his belt and showed his white teeth in a grin as the two men dismounted at the tie-rail, hitched the horses and mounted the three step to the porch.

'Tom Selby in?' asked Corrigan politely.

He got an answer in an insolent drawl. 'Nope. Why? Who the hell are you?'

'Bill Corrigan of the Double C. This is my top hand Sam Hicks. Now will you tell me where I can find Tom Selby?'

'Corrigan, huh? I've heard of you. Yuh should be dead, hombre. Any man who tangles with Hogan should be dead.'

'Maybe. Now quite beating your gums. Where's Selby?'

'Cuttin' timber—if he isn't dead by now!' was the reply.

Chapter Seven

Bill Corrigan stared at the runty young gunman and allowed his complete dislike for this breed of man to show on his face. The man was probably about twenty-two years of age, small-framed, cocky as hell, a small man in all respects except in the handling of a gun. Corrigan's eyes dropped to the holstered weapon and noted the rosewood butt, the oiled leather in which it lay. He looked up again at white teeth in a thin face— teeth that sneered. A soft down of blond hair covered the man's chin and light hair under the pushed-back hat showed thick and wavy. The man's whole stance was one of challenge and insult.

'You seem mighty interested in that word,' murmured Bill Corrigan.

'What word? You ribbin' me?'

'The word is "dead", pal. You've said it three times already. You interested in being dead?'

Colour rose under the young gunman's golden tan. 'Yuh're being funny, huh?'

Corrigan inched closer and grinned more of his dislike. 'Funny as hell. When I asked you a question about Tom Selby I expected a sane reply. Now what do you mean by he's cuttin' timber if he isn't dead by now? What would make a smart little feller like you talk like that?'

'Lissen you!' snarled the other man. 'The hell with you an' the hell with Selby! He's out cuttin' timber an' he's due to meet with an accident.'

'Is that so? Boy, I don't like you!'

Corrigan was close enough. He had twice the weight and strength of this hired gunny, even though he had been ill, and he used it without compunction.

Two hands chopped out in short jabs that struck at the nose and eyes of the derisive, wary face before him. It was like hacking at a mask. The man had not expected the attack. His eyes widened in pain as his head jerked right and then left. Too late his body twisted in an effort to dodge back. Corrigan's hands cut down again, palms open, the bony edges of hard muscle chopping at the face. Blood spurted from the man's nose and then his legs activated him and his body twisted out of immediate reach. A hand shot to his holster but was stopped by a bigger hand that tightened like a brutal, bone crushing vice. Corrigan's hand.

And then the small gunman lost his weapon—his one asset in a world that acknowledged the supremacy of a man with a fast Colt. The gun thudded twice as it bounced down the porch steps.

Corrigan stepped back so that his arm could travel with some velocity. His fist rammed out and hit the gunman right in the mouth. Knuckles ground on the nice white teeth and probably slacked some. Lips burst unpleasantly. Another fist was travelling quickly at the same time and it exploded between the man's eyes.

Corrigan was through with being nice.

As the man sagged to the porch, Corrigan turned away. He was finished with this hired man. His temple throbbed again. He felt completely brutalized and he realized it was a cloak he would have to wear from now on until this thing was finished. He turned to Sam Hicks.

'You heard what he said about Tom Selby?'

'I heard.'

'Let's go.'

'And those other two gents—Blue Pete and his mate, Nat?'

'I haven't forgotten.'

They got the horses, mounted them and rode through the lumber camp. A few of the hired labour stared, loggers paid to work and mind their own affairs. Corrigan did not know them. At the moment he did not need their help. The important thing was to locate Tom Selby.

Before the 'accident' happened!

The whine of a sawmill screeched out suddenly as the blade cut into some new logs. A great wagon, with wheels of solid oak, rolled down the gradient, drawn by a team of four big horses. Chains clinked with the timber frame of the great wagon as it bore down with its load of giant cedar boles. Higher up the hill there was a stream of mountain water, dammed at some point and diverted into a sluice made of halved pine logs. Corrigan stared into the sun, sitting tall and big on the jigging horse. Somewhere up that hill it seemed likely Tom Selby was working. Cutting timber! He had not cut timber for a long time. He had plenty of hired hands for that. What sort of lousy setup was working in this camp! Who had forced Tom Selby to work in the forest? He was supposed to be the boss.

The horses picked a quick way up the trail. The narrow track was wide enough for a goat, and on both sides the undergrowth was thick around the trees. It was mostly pine and juniper thickets but occasionally a big cedar stood high into the sky and in odd clumps a few oaks gripped the ground with gnarled roots. Corrigan and Sam Hicks went past clearings where logger squads were using keen axes to good effect. They passed a great mountain of piled branches and came to a clearway where a big horse was hauling single logs. Corrigan stopped the man holding the lead leathers of the hauler.

'Where's Mr Selby? Have you seen him?'

The hefty red-whiskered man stared curiously. 'Shore. He's higher up the gradient.'

'Why is he cutting logs? Do you know?'

The man spat. 'I'm paid to haul, mister.'

'Yeah? Who gives you orders?'

'We got a gang boss. He's new.'

'Is he? Has he got a name?'

'I call him a bastard! He's known as Bat Grayson. Anythin' else?'

'Where is Bat Grayson?'

The man jerked his head. 'As it happens, he's right up there with Tom Selby—an' I can tell you it's Grayson that's giving the orders. Me, I ain't stickin' around here much longer. I'll git my time an' move on. I don't like what I see around hyar, an' that's fer shore.'

'What's wrong?'

The red-haired man glared up to Corrigan. 'Reckon yuh know! Otherwise why're yuh so all-fired curious! Another thing—jest take a look at them no-good rannigans thet's supposed to be workin' with Selby.'

'What's wrong with them?'

'Wrong? Hell, they don't work! I don't get it! A big fat bastard called Blue Pete an' a little rat by the name o' Nat! Jest imagine, mister, them no-goods git paid the same as me!'

'Thanks, friend,' muttered Corrigan. 'I'll see you again. Stick around. This job will need good men again pretty soon. An' yuh won't be working for this Bat Grayson.'

'Thet bastard!' said the man again.

They jigged the horses a bit further up the steeply rising track and Sam Hicks muttered: 'Now that hombre sure don't like this Bat Grayson feller!'

They could not see very far in the thick forest. And so they came to a clearing without warning. And in a second Bill Corrigan took in a lot of things.

He saw four men. One was Tom Selby, alive but facing death. Sitting on a fallen tree bole was a big fat man wearing worn bucksins. His dark face and high cheekbones at once denoted Indian blood. His flat nose and slitted mouth was truly representative of the breed. He sat and switched a pliant twig at the grass and undergrowth. He wore a gun but there was little indication that he was proud of the weapon for the holster was worn and cracked and the gun butt chipped and dull.

Corrigan mentally figured that this was Bat Grayson. He had a cold stare fixed on two other men, who were working. Bill was sure these men were Blue Pete and Nat. They were chipping away with gleaming axes at a large pine and were half-way through the cut. They worked like two incompetents, the worst loggers he had ever seen. Blue Pete was a man with a black beard. His dirty undershirt was stained with blood and food and plain dirt. He was twice the size of his side-kick, Nat. This person was a rat-faced individual whose pants and shirt seemed to big for him.

As for Tom Selby, his wrists were roped together and he was tethered to a tree stump like some animal. The rope would allow him to move about three feet either to right or left. This was not much scope to dodge a falling tree, something that would fall like a black giant from the sky and crush a frail human body.

That seemed to be the incredible plan, for Blue Pete and Nat were hacking at a tree that was lined up to fall directly on the spot where Tom Selby was tethered. As Bill Corrigan and Sam Hicks appeared through the screen of trees, the two no-goods stopped working to stare with gaping mouths.

The half-breed swivelled on the tree bole and quit

swishing his length of springy branch. He stared, his slit mouth and cold eyes truly Indian.

Tom Selby uttered a rasping cry and attempted to move forward. 'Corrigan!' he pleaded.

Bill Corrigan's gun came steadily into his hand. It pointed first at Bat Grayson and then at Blue Pete and Nat.

'The first one,' said Bill coldly, 'who wants to try for gunplay should put his name on the list now. You two—Blue Pete an' Nat, ain't it?'

The two drifters looked at each other. The axe handles seemed to have stuck to their hands with fear and sweat.

'Two handy gents with tar torches,' stated Corrigan. 'Remember my ranch buildings?'

Another glance passed between the two men and they slowly straightened. Corrigan noted they were not wearing guns. All the same an urge to punish these two swine rose from somewhere in his guts and stuck sourly in his throat. He felt his hand tighten around his gun. So these two were the filthy, low arsonists who had destroyed his ranch buildings—two men who were incapable themselves of building anything better than a deck of cards in a saloon!

'Sam, cut Tom Selby loose,' he grated. 'I've got this lot covered. It'll be a pleasure if they try anythin'.'

Sam nodded. A few minutes fast work with his knife and Tom Selby was free. The two men returned to Sam's horse. Selby rubbed his wrists and tried to suppress the shakes in his limbs. Sam Hicks rolled a cigarette and handed it to the lumberman and lit it.

Bill Corrigan had been eyeing Bat Grayson. The man sat motionless on the log. The Indian in him showed clearly in his passive manner and his lack of emotion. His ugly face was shaded by a battered hat. The uncared for gun lay solidly in the indifferent holster. The plaint twig he held did not move.

'Git up!' snapped Bill Corrigan. 'On your feet.'

The man rose slowly, came to his full height. He was big and he was fat. He reminded Corrigan of a lot of bit fat men he had known who could work like blazes and move swiftly when needed.

'Yuh're a Cassidy man,' said Bill. 'You were figurin' to kill Tom Selby. If that tree fell on him it could be made to look like an accident. Yuh could bring a couple of reliable men up to take a look at the setup an' they'd be able to testify that he'd been killed by a falling tree. I suppose that would leave the Cassidy boyos free to move in here an' take over lock, stock and barrel.'

The man did not speak.

'You can go for your gun—anytime!' Corrigan's words slurred out in moment of savage resentment at this man and all he stood for.

Bat Grayson did not move. Corrigan holstered his gun.

'Just to make it even,' he lipped.

The scar on his temple throbbed again as his anger seethed. If he was edgy he was also itching for action. Right now he was full of hatred. Up to date it was not

94

a quality he had admired in any man, but maybe there were times when it was right to hate.

'You scared to go for that gun!' he mocked the big fat man.

The man spoke in a deep voice. 'I don't know you. Ride out. I don't go fer gunplay.'

'Jest little murderous setups for your bosses!' snarled Corrigan. 'Aw right—you two!' He swung to Blue Pete and the little man. 'Go git his gun. Any one o' you! Git his gun.'

Blue Pete muttered something under his breath.

'I didn't hear yuh,' said Corrigan. 'If yuh want to insult me, go git that big fat feller's gun and then make a play. You two set fire to my ranch.'

The little rat-faced man known as Nat started to protest. 'Wasn't us, mister! Where'd you get that? Wasn't me—nossir! I wouldn't do a thing like that!'

Blue Pete added something in an earnest growl that Corrigan did not understand. Corrigan's eyes glinted in a new surge of anger. His hand flashed and his gun appeared again. Bue Pete and Nat visibly cowered. Bat Grayson stood in true Indian immobility.

'Sam,' said Corrigan in a voice that shook, 'git that feller's gun and throw it away. Before I kill this lousy lot in cold blood.'

Sam Hicks nodded. However, he took no chances with Bat Grayson. The man was an unknown quality. Somewhere in that passive frame there was cunning and trickery, he was sure of that. The lumber hauler had been sure of his assessment, and, anyway, this man had been hand-picked by Sep and Clark Cassidy.

He took the battered gun from the dilapidated holster and threw it away. He stepped back; got to his horse again.

'You lot—start walkin'!' rasped Bill Corrigan. 'Back to the camp. Tom!' He called to the lumberman. 'Git up behind me.'

Slowly, the cavalcade set off. Bill Corrigan broke his grim silence and said: 'Tom, what in hell is the matter? How come the Cassidys can steamroll you out of your property?'

'It's a long story,' said a tired voice behind him. 'I— I'll tell you everything—later—when we hit the camp—'

'Tell me now.'

'I need a drink. I—I—don't feel good, Bill. I'm not the man you think I am. I—I—I'm bein' blackmailed!'

'That figures.'

'I—I—I'll tell you more later.'

'They want to get rid of you—permanently. Yuh know that.'

'I know it, Bill. But—hell, I don't want to talk about it—just yet!' And Tom Selby almost groaned.

Clear of the timber, they rode into the lumber camp and got some curious glances from a few men who stopped working to look up. Bat Grayson and the other two walked ahead of Corrigan and Sam Hicks. Blue Pete and Nat were arguing earnestly in low tones and casting dubious glances at Corrigan every few yards of traversed ground.

Sam Hicks looked inquiringly at Corrigan.

'What d'yuh figure to do with this bunch?'

'I'm runnin' them off this property—for a start. Those two jaspers who fired my ranch can go to the jail and wait for a trial—an' if Dan Holladay won't agree to that maybe the U.S. Marshal from Laramie will have different ideas.'

A groan came from Tom Selby. 'What's this about the U.S. Marshal?'

'I've sent for him, Tom.'

'Oh, God! I'm finished—licked!'

'What's wrong? Are yuh scared to meet the Marshal?'

But Tom Selby was miserably silent. They dismounted at the camp office, and Selby hurried inside. When Bill Corrigan entered the place, the lumberman was pouring a drink with shaking hands. He set the bottle down on the desk top and mumbled: 'Help yourself, Bill.'

'Nope. Are yuh goin' to talk, Tom?'

'I—I—'

'Hurry it up. Sam Hicks is keeping a gun on those three no-goods.'

'Well—you might as well know the truth. Clark Cassidy has a hold on me all right—you must guess that. He knows plenty about me and can prove it all.'

'Yeah?'

'I'm wanted for murder,' said Tom Selby dully. 'I killed a man five years ago—gettin' on six years when I think about it—and Clark Cassidy can put the law on me just like that!' Tom Selby snapped his fingers slowly. 'Don't make any mistake, Bill. I killed that man. It was

97

over a woman. Huh—she was some woman! A lovely double-crossing little lady! We lived together—oh, I wanted to marry her. She wasn't so sure. As I see it now, she was aimin' for a galoot with more money.' Tom Selby turned his back. 'I went out one night and killed that man, Corrigan. I was mad with jealousy—I can't make you understand—I was just crazy. I went to see him, fought with him and killed him. I rode out of that town.'

'And Cassidy can slick the law on you?'

'He can. And he will. Unless I hand this place to him.'

'Seems like he wasn't satisfied with that,' said Corrigan grimly. 'He wanted you out of the way permanently.'

'I'm finished.'

'How come Clark Cassidy knows so much about the killing?'

A grim laugh sounded from Tom Selby. 'He was one of the lady's admirers himself! He knew everythin'. He knew her friends. He knows the lawmen back there who are still looking for me!'

Corrigan turned. 'Stick around, Tom. Maybe it will be hell—but there's nothin' else to do. Don't run.'

'I guess I've got to think—'

Bill Corrigan went out to Sam Hicks.

'These jaspers are gittin' mighty restless,' commented Sam, 'an' I ain't so happy myself. I've been holding this gun for a long time.'

'We're going, Sam.' Bill Corrigan brought his gun out and walked close to Bat Grayson. 'Yuh can git clear out o' this territory, man, an' if I see you again I'll—'

He never finished the warning. The challenge that hurled at him came from his left in the shape of a voice filled with malice.

'You—Corrigan!' The two words were thick with hate. Corrigan wheeled like an oiled spindle; saw the runty young gunman and his pointed gun. Guns spoke as if linked by some telegraph system. The bark of exploding Colts cut the air and brought all thought and action to one point of immediacy.

Corrigan was not sure how he beat the gunman. There was no explaining a second of desperate action. His reaction had been faster than thought; as quick as jagged lightning.

In fact, surprise hit him when he saw the young gunman slowly crumple, fold inch by inch, as if his guts were seared by sudden pain. But when he did hit the earth and his gun slithered from him, it was not because of trouble with his guts. There was a gunshot hole in his head and blood was already trickling out.

Another corpse, thought Corrigan. Another gun hireling who had met the only fate he could expect from a man who toted guns for a living.

Bat Grayson was backing from the spot, his big fat body seemingly balanced warily on legs that wanted to get away fast from this spot. Blue Pete and Nat were frozen figures, like silhouettes to Corrigan's quickly flickering eyes.

Sam Hicks growled up to him. 'You all right?'

'It missed me. Nearly nicked my ear.'

Sam Hicks went to the horses, pacified them. In the meantime, a few men slowly approached and looked down at the dead young gunny. There were no expressions of concern. One man even spat. Another went back to his job. A third stared at Bill Corrigan, flicked a glance at Blue Pete and Nat and then backed away and stared again.

Tom Selby sidled out of the office and took one look at the dead man. He stared as if disbelieving. Fear was chased out of his face by an expression of satisfaction.

'What the hell!' he muttered. 'He got what he asked for. Wish I'd had the guts to kill him myself—blasted little upstart!'

'Lug him into the office,' snapped Corrigan.

'Why? He's just a damned animal. Throw him in a hole.'

'He's a dead human being,' said Bill Corrigan. 'Yuh're boss around here, Tom. Give some orders. Get that man buried.'

'Sure. Like the Cassidys wanted to bury me—under a two ton tree bole!'

'Get him buried,' repeated Corrigan.

Bat Grayson was running now, big legs taking him past a big stack of logs. Corrigan watched him go and grimly considered that his man was probably another new enemy. He would have to be reckoned with. He had a feeling the man would employ cunning in any action he might take.

Words were babbling from Nat's thin rat face. 'Say—

I didn't—want to fire yore ranch—nossir! I—I—wasn't there—warn't me! Sure warn't!'

Blue Pete suddenly wiped the back of his hand over his side-kick's mouth. 'Jest button yore lip! Don't know why I haul yuh around, yuh yellow little varmint! Why yuh're—'

'Shut up!' Corrigan rapped. He turned to Tom Selby. 'How about some horses? I'm taking these two rats into town.'

'To thet durned sheriff?' sneered Blue Pete. 'Heh! I bin in worse jails! Heh!'

Nat laughed eagerly in unison with his partner. 'Shore, we ain't worried about thet jail—'

Blue Pete kicked him. 'Shaddap!'

'You'll worry,' stated Corrigan. 'I'm taking the key when yuh hit that jail. And you'll deal with the U.S. Marshal from Laramie when he gits here.'

He was suddenly sick of talk. He held a gun on the two drifters while Sam Hicks got horses. Within fifteen minutes the two worthless characters were hoisted into saddles and their hands tied in front of them. The little man, Nat, maintained a constant stream of futile protestations of innocence, excuses and contradictions. His partner growled and swore and periodically stared at Bill Corrigan with cunning eyes.

Fed up with these two scum, Corrigan rode in silence for a long time and as Sam Hicks was not the type to chatter there was little exchange of plans. They rode down from the forests, into the rolling hills and plains, and eventually descended into the town. By that time they were two hungry men.

'We'll eat when we get rid o' these two,' stated Bill Corrigan. 'An' maybe we'll pick up Bert Foggin.'

On the boardwalks, loungers stared at the oddly assorted riders. They passed the burnt-out remains of the Cassidy office and Corrigan hardly smiled. They came to the sheriff's office and dismounted. Corrigan and Sam Hicks pulled the two skunks from the horses and marched them on to the wooden porch.

'Now we'll see how the sheriff reacts to this!' muttered Bill Corrigan.

The four men made a bit of noise as they crowded into the office and Corrigan was occupied handling Blue Pete.

Then when he stared at Sheriff Holladay, he became instantly aware of another man. The icy tingle of total awareness flooded him. The gunman Hogan was sitting at the sheriff's desk!

Chapter Eight

'Make yourself at home, hombres,' said Hogan with a smile. He tilted the office chair a little but that was his only movement. He continued to smile. This facial expression lay falsely on his white face and thin lips. It did not fade. It seemed the luxury of a smile did not happen very often.

The Corrigan saw the reason for the smile. The man was wearing a deputy badge pinned to his black shirt.

'Ah,' murmured Corrigan. Then he stared again into the black eyes and saw no smile there. Instead, he got an indescribable feeling of probing into twin pits of cold hate. This was the inner being of a man who wanted him dead.

'You've been promoted,' stated Bill Corrigan. 'Waal, you're not the first gunman turned law. Usually, though, there is genuine reform. You upholdin' the law now, Hogan?'

The smile did not fade. The chair tilted again.

'He's a duly appointed deputy!' shrilled Dan Holladay. He was hatless and his thin hair was ruffled.

'Yeah. Things change around here—that's so.' Corrigan moved slowly. 'I've been out of circulation—but yuh know that.'

'You've mended well,' said Hogan. 'Seems you've been well looked after.'

'Who patched you up?' asked Corrigan insolently. 'I didn't think yuh had any friends!'

Hogan got gently to his feet. Bill's eyes flicked down. The man was wearing the twin Colts.

'I've got all the friends I want,' said Hogan. 'Nice seein' you, Corrigan. We'll meet up again pretty soon,' he added significantly.

Damn you, thought Corrigan, you lousy inhuman gunny! So okay, we'll meet again. And hell will take you!

Aloud he said: 'I've got some of Cassidy men right here, as yuh can see. I want them jailed. I want the key, too. They set fire to my ranch. I'm gonna prove it when the U.S. Marshal from Laramie hits town.'

'You can't do this!' shouted Dan Holladay. The man's nerves seemed close to breaking point. 'Yuh got no proof. Damn! I'm the sheriff around here—'

'Act like one.' Corrigan pushed Blue Pete across the office. 'I'm tellin' yuh to jail this man—and his partner! I'll supply the proof.'

'Stick them in the hoosegow, Holladay,' said Hogan easily. 'Maybe that will make Mister Corrigan happy. After all, he ain't got so long to live an' he's got a right to be happy.'

Corrigan glanced at the man, up and down, a grim

stare that memorized little details like the new nick in the man's leather belt.

'I don't want them in the jail—' began the sheriff.

'Aw, stick them in,' drawled Hogan. 'They need a rest. From what I hear, they've bin workin' up in that lumber camp. It's hard work, Holladay, cuttin' timber.'

The little man, Nat, seemed galvanized into speech again. Words rattled from his lips. . . .

'Say . . . you know . . . thet young gunslinger up at the camp . . . he's dead. Corrigan killed him!'

Hogan stiffened and caution moulded into his face. At that moment there was little chance of his smile returning.

Sheriff Dan Holladay looked nonplussed. Then, uneasily: 'I—I—take it that was a fair fight, Corrigan?'

'Yuh can take it.'

Nat yapped again, eager to be of service. 'He chased that gang boss outa the place—yuh know that Bat Grayson galoot.'

'I don't know anything about that man,' said Holladay hurriedly.

'Yuh've been busy, Corrigan,' said Hogan. 'The Cassidy brothers will like this, not much! Waal, it won't matter. I guess there's always another day.'

'D'yuh figure you're playin' with me?' Bill Corrigan asked bluntly. 'You seem to be gettin' some satisfaction out o' fooling along.'

'It is interestin' wondering when I should kill you.'

Corrigan nodded. 'I quit beating my gums. Sheriff, I want these galoots jailed—now. I'll get proof of their guilt. One of them is ready to confess. When the U.S. Marshal hits town, he'll git Judge Hendricks to hold court . . .'

'You fool!' The sheriff trembled. 'The U.S. Marshal won't get here! Hogan an' me cancelled yore message!'

Once again Hogan smiled, and he nodded. 'Say, Dan, you should ha' kept that bit to yourself.'

'I'm sick of his meddlin'!'

'Then yuh're goin' to be a damnsight sicker!' rumbled Corrigan and his gun leaped to his hand. Instinct and anger had stabbed him into this situation. He had had no intention of drawing on Holladay and Hogan and there were two good reasons; he did not want to die on the end of twin Colts and, in fact, these two men were wearing lawman's badges. But the gun was out, a reality, and there was no backing down now.

'Git them two rannies in the jail—pronto—an' hand me the key!' rapped Corrigan.

Sheriff Holladay spluttered and jerked his eyes from the gun to Corrigan's eyes and then back to the gun. He was lost for words. Hogan maintained his smile.

'Sam—lock them two up an' keep the key,' directed Bill Corrigan.

Sam Hicks picked the big bunch of keys from a hook on the wall, opened a jail door. With a grim look at Hogan, he took out his gun and prodded the two drifters into the jail.

Blue Pete and Nat were shoved into the jail and the door was locked. Sensing some safety behind bars, the two drifters started to abuse Corrigan and Sam Hicks, especially Nat, the bony little man, who switched from pleading to some pretty low obscenities. Sam Hicks handed the keys to Bill Corrigan. The sheriff feebly stuck his nose in here.

'That's town property . . . gimme those keys . . .'

Corrigan rattled the big steel keys. 'If you figure to set them two free, you'll have to cut the lock. That will mess up some more town property an' take up a lot of yore time. An' thanks for tellin' me about the U.S. Marshal.'

He and Sam Hicks moved slowly to the office outer door. Hogan was still smiling, like a man who figures he has all the aces. Corrigan took a chance and holstered his gun. His fingers tingled as his hand stayed near the holster, but Hogan smiled pleasantly—and a bit thoughtfully.

Corrigan paused grimly at the door. 'There's other ways of reachin' the U.S. Marshal at Laramie. A good rider could hit the town in two days.'

He left the two men and in a couple of seconds he was out on the street. He turned to Sam Hicks.

'It's anybody's guess how long those two rannies will be in that jail.'

'Hogan played it smooth.'

'Yeah. He likes to chose the time an' place. C'mon, let's eat, Sam.'

They led the four horses along the main stem and noted the town was full of the usual bustle and activity. The stage was in and unloading passengers—one oldish woman in bonnet and bustle, a gent in a city suit, an

107

old-timer from some place north. The driver went into the depot with the mail-bags. The four-in-hand champed on frothy bits and steam rose from their hides.

Women were on the boardwalks, going to stores. The ring of a hammer on an anvil came from the smithy. Two carpenters hammered nails into a new clapboard building. Overhead the sun hung full and hot in a cloudless sky.

They hitched the animals outside an eat-house and went in. Pretty soon they were silently enjoying steak and beans and fried potatoes, large helpings, and the only condiment was salt.

'Boss, what d'yuh aim to do now?'

'Work. There's nothing to do but go back to the spread and git some work started.'

Sam nodded thoughtfully.

Bill Corrigan paused again in his eating. 'What else is there to do? Now don't talk like thet old lobo, Bert Foggin! He figures I should go kill the Cassidy brothers, Hogan, Blue Pete an' Nat—an' anybody else who gits in the way! Just like that. This is supposed to be a law abiding town, Sam.'

'It used to be.'

'Yeah. Waal, it will be again.'

'All the same,' said Sam, 'if they come gunnin' for yuh, I reckon you'll shoot. Maybe that's the way the score will be settled.' He paused. 'I'll be with yuh.'

Corrigan grinned. 'Good. Say, wonder if old Bert Foggin is still in town!'

They were out in the street again some time later and

they stashed two of the horses in a livery and mounted their own. The animals plodded slowly down the dusty main stem and came to the Broken Horseshoe Saloon. One glance at the new saloon on the other side of the road and Bill Corrigan saw that it was doing a good trade. Horses were standing at the tie-rail. A hubbub of voices could be heard from the road. It seemed there was a contingent of cowpokes in town and most of them were in the new saloon. Maybe they were gambling away their hard-earned wages. Corrigan looked at the newly painted sign—GOLD NUGGET. Well, it seemed that was true enough—for the Cassidy brothers. The building had been pushed up fast and some of the unpainted boards were very new. Apparently, the Cassidy brothers could find finance for their schemes. How much they owed to some bank was anybody's guess.

Corrigan had a mental picture of his own property standing black and gaunt against the green plain and the background of rolling hills. He stared bitterly at the new building. Its very existence was an affront. Probably Clark and Sep Cassidy were on the premises right now and they would be conducting their other 'business' from the place. The loss of their smaller office was obviously no great worry. So these damned skunks were prospering!

They paused so long in the saddle that Sam Hicks stared inquiringly at his boss, guessing at his thoughts. He had never seen Bill Corrigan so bitter. He had always known his employer as a fair man, a man of even temper and an ability to reason and see another point

109

of view. And now events were forcing this man to neglect his work as a rancher and go out gunning. Well, he had a partner! They would see this thing through. If Bill Corrigan wanted work done, they would work. If he figured to gun-hunt some human coyotes, they would do just that.

As they sat thoughtfully on saddle-leather, they saw Sheriff Dan Holladay walk swiftly up the main stem. He seemed to hesitate when he noticed Corrigan and Sam Hicks on their patient mustangs, and then he increased his pace again and dived into the Gold Nugget. Corrigan had noticed he was wearing a new hat—a genuine J.B. Stetson—and his gun lay in a polished holster.

'Gone to tell the Cassidy boyos the latest news,' remarked Bill Corrigan.

'Like how the young gunny is buzzard bait,' said Sam Hicks. 'An' Bat Grayson has been run off the lumber camp.'

Corrigan nodded. 'That an' other things. As for Bat Grayson, he'll just git new orders from Sep or Clark. Maybe we'll tangle again.'

'I guess so,' admitted Sam Hicks.

'Nothin' is settled,' said Corrigan grimly. 'We need men up at Tom Selby's place to make sure Bat Grayson doesn't take over again, but we ain't got men or time. Maybe I'll ride up again tomorrow.'

He knew he was one man against many, and he was spending time on matters that were not ranching. Stolen stock and burnt out buildings represented a big loss to him. So far he was losing out to the Cassidy brothers and he did not like the feeling. True he had fouled up their plans to some extent but not enough.

He broke off his thought with a snap of decision.

'Let's go inside this dump,' he said. 'Have a drink on me, Sam. I'm tired of bein' pushed around. Let's see what we can stir up.'

Sam nodded, a half-smile on his square, honest face. They hitched the horses to the tie rail. Sam followed Corrigan through the bat-wings.

The usual stuffy air of a saloon hit them but that was little concern. The place was full of cow-pokes. A piano in a corner was being hammered by a shirt-sleeved virtuoso who, incredibly, was wooing the crowd of drunks with 'Beautiful Dreamer' and making a hack of it. Almost a quarter of the big room was taken up with tables at which poker was being played and there were plenty of men grim-faced and intent upon the game. The house stood to collect a good percentage, as was usual, but Corrigan had Ed Hunter's word that this was no limit gambling and probably crooked. At the end of the long saloon lay a raised stage complete with curtains and a grand piano and space for any other musicians that may be found. The place was a replica of scores of saloons to be found throughout the west and should have been in a position to make money without resorting to crooked methods.

Corrigan and Sam pushed up to the bar and secured a beer each. Bottles were plentiful on the polished pine counter—a cheap brand of whisky known as Colonel

Gregg. Corrigan and Sam Hicks looked around. He noted first that the sheriff was not to be seen.

It was a fair bet there were private rooms at the back. Maybe Dan Holladay was somewhere back telling the tale. By his actions it seemed the sheriff favoured Sep and Clark Cassidy, probably because he realized they held power. The next step would be for him to accept bribes and then he would be totally under the Cassidy brothers' influence. If it got that far!

Corrigan's quick glances around the saloon soon lighted on the immaculately dressed man who appeared from the back rooms and wended a swift way through the customers.

'Howdy, Mr Hunter,' murmured Bill Corrigan, halting the man.

For a moment Ed Hunter paused, his good-looking face setting into a blank mask. Only his eyes flickered.

'Good day, sir,' he muttered softly and then stepped lithely to one side and moved through the saloon.

'Now that galoot sure didn't want to stop long,' commented Sam Hicks.

'It figures,' said Corrigan. 'He's on the Cassidy payroll. Pretty soon I'll see our friend again—an' I think the conversation will be a mite longer than that!'

He took a gulp at his beer. Sam followed his example. Corrigan put his glass down with a slam.

'Let's git! Let's quit foolin' around here.'

Angrily, he began to shove forward and a few men stared. With Sam Hicks he went through the batwings and hit the street. With quick movement they unhitched the horses and climbed aboard. They cantered away, silent, moody.

They turned the block of buildings where the bank occupied a corner site and were passing an alley between two buildings when they heard the sharp command.

'Corrigan—here!'

Bill Corrigan's head turned as his hand flashed to his gun, sheer instinct making the play, but his hand stayed on the leather when he saw the speaker.

'Hunter! What do you want?'

'I want to speak to you. I hurried down here to intercept you.'

Corrigan and Sam Hicks jigged the horse into the alley where few would see them on the main street.

'Well?' prompted Corrigan.

Ed Hunter's face took on a careful look. 'I've heard about you killing the gunman up at the lumber camp and chasing Bat Grayson. Holladay has been talking to Sep and Clark. They've told Hogan to get you good and final.'

'That figures.'

'Of course, it will be legal now that Hogan is a deputy ...'

'Sure thing,' agreed Corrigan. 'Yuh ain't tellin' me anything I don't know.'

'They have deeds prepared concerning Selby's lumber camp and by some means which I do not know about they can buy the place from under him at a very low valuation.'

113

'Yep. I know.'

'But those two devils want the place for less than that. Now if Selby were to die the place might be sold at auction and they might lose it to another buyer. I've found out that Selby has made out a document which gives his place to Sep and Clark Cassidy in the event of his death—a sort of will. It's incredible, but I've seen the document. The fool has signed his own death warrant.'

'Seeing yuh know so much,' grated Bill Corrigan, 'I can tell yuh more. Tom Selby is being blackmailed by yore two lobo employers. That's all I'm tellin' you.'

'That man's life is in danger.'

Corrigan nodded grimly. 'Seems there's only one thing to do.'

'What's that?'

'Kill those two Cassidy snakes.'

'That would be murder—and you'd hang.'

'Yep. I get the point. Now tell me where yuh fit in.'

'I'll tell you—pretty soon.' Ed Hunter hesitated. Then he opened his expensive jacket. Corrigan flashed a glance at the holster strapped around him. 'I can tell you I carry a gun.'

'What does that mean?'

'It means I'm ready,' said Ed Hunter.

'I get the feelin' that yuh don't really like the Cassidy brothers very much,' said Corrigan slowly.

'Never seen a gent hedge so much,' commented Sam Hicks unexpectedly.

'You may be glad of my help someday,' said the other man enigmatically.

And with that last remark he walked quickly away. Bill Corrigan and Sam Hicks jigged the horses back into the main street again and rode slowly along. Corrigan was deep in thought. Ed Hunter had reminded him that Tom Selby was still in great danger. Killing the young gunny and running off Bat Grayson had not solved anything. But what was the next step? It was impossible to guard Tom Selby night and day! And what about Hogan? He was commissioned to kill. Not only was he hired, but the man had a personal score to settle. His confidence in his skill was so high, he would undoubtedly manufacture the confrontation pretty soon. Then there was the menace of Bat Grayson. It was difficult to estimate what sort of move he might make. But Corrigan had a feeling this man would strike—in his own way.

'Sam, I reckon it might be a good idea if yuh rode up to Tom Selby's place and got him to leave that damned lumber camp for a few days. Ask him if he'll ride with yuh to the Double C. He can stick around the ranch for some time while we git some building work done— that way we'll know he's safe. Can yuh do that for me, Sam?'

'Sure thing. I'll head for those hills right away. I'll tell that galoot what yuh propose, boss.'

Corrigan nodded. They rode out of town together and then parted. Thoughtfully, he watched Sam's horse disappear and then he began a canter back to the Double C.

He would just have to get some real work done.

When he finally set eyes on the charred remains of his ranch buildings again, the grim in-bitten feeling rose from his guts and he felt an itch to kill someone for this. Then he heard a shout; whipped around to see old Bert Foggin emerge from behind the charred and ruined barn.

'Say, boss, I bin workin'—clearing away the durned muck.'

'Good. Wish that blasted timber would arrive.'

Corrigan did work. Three hours of fast, definite activity resulted in a small wickiup, made from corral poles and other fencing undamaged by fire. It was big enough to shelter two or three men and take their saddles and bedrolls. It was terribly small compared to the solid ranch-house that had stood on this land, but it would have to serve. When Sam Hicks returned, he thought, they'd have to start work in earnest, maybe at sunup next day, and take an assessment of the cattle in the hills and draws. He needed another hand on the place. He wondered where Li Foo and the other waddy had got to. Probably they were doing casual work in West Plains, scared or disinclined to return to the Double C.

As the sun fell and dusk crept over the quiet hills they got a fire going, and in the cheerful glow the two men felt a certain satisfaction. They were close to the land and this was home. Bert was cooking grub when they heard the sound of approaching hoofs.

Corrigan was waiting for the dim figures to become real and identifiable, thumbs hooked in his gunbelt and eyes narrowed, and when he finally made out Sam Hicks he gave a grunt. He had seen that the other man was Tom Selby.

'I brought him out, like yuh said, boss!'

'So yuh're still alive, Tom,' commented Bill Corrigan.

The lumberman swung down stiffly from his blowing horse and pushed his hat back to reveal his silver hair. 'Yeah. But for how long?'

'I've learnt some things, Tom,' said Corrigan. 'That damned document yuh signed makin' over your place to the Cassidys in the event of your death—that was a damnfool thing to do!'

'You sure get to know things!' muttered Tom Selby. He stared at Corrigan and at Sam Hicks and Bert Foggin. Fear etched new lines in his face.

'Why'd yuh sign it?'

'You know why,' snapped the other irritably. 'They were pressin' me to sign this and that. I just figured to stall. I thought maybe they were bluffing. . . .'

'They've got hired killers,' stated Corrigan, 'And they're greedy.' He gestured to the burnt ranch-yard. 'Just look at this. They dared to do this. Always with hired rannigans—I wish to God they'd come gunnin' themselves. I'd know how to deal with that. They want power. They want this ranch and your lumber camp—an' anything else they can buy or cheat in West Plains. They must be taking big chances to consolidate their power—an' that means they can be toppled.' He paused. 'The best way would be a slug. . . .'

'You wouldn't kill in cold blood,' said Tom Selby tiredly. 'Hell—the best thing I kin do is ride out of here at sunup and keep on riding. God knows I've got good enough reasons!'

He broke off the talk by leading his horse to the undamaged corral. When he returned to the fire and wickiup with his saddle and gear, he stared around.

'Hell, Corrigan, they've got you beat, too!'

'I'm going to rebuild!' rapped the other.

'If they let you. If you stay alive. . . .'

'Sit down and rest, Tom. Yuh need it. Have some coffee—old Bert made it an' it's good. In the morning you'll feel better. We'll figure out somethin'.'

'I'm figuring out something now,' was Tom Selby's curious answer. He brought some paper from inside a pocket in his flapping vest. 'I guess you don't have pen and ink on hand in this primitive place, Corrigan—so it'll have to be done with a pencil. I happen to have one right with me.' He brought out the thick brown stick. 'Latest lead writing pencil . . . now let me see . . .'

'What the devil have yuh in mind?' Bill Corrigan asked.

He watched in silence as the lumberman sat down near the fire and wrote slowly in a fine hand on the paper. Sam and Bert watched curiously. When finally Tom Selby handed the sheet of paper to them for their signatures, old Bert Foggin spluttered.

'Say . . . I ain't so good at writin' an' readin' . . . I

118

reckon I kin sign my name but what in blazes am I being a witness fer?'

'You tell him, Sam?' said Tom Selby.

Sam Hicks read with some difficulty. Then: 'Waal, ah, um, you're as good as sayin' right here on this paper that yuh aim to hand over the lumber camp an' all its— ah—um—business to Bill Corrigan of the Double C in the—ah—event of yore death—an' this—this document —what's this word—supercedes any other!'

'Yep. Now you two sign it.'

Corrigan gripped Tom's arm. 'Yuh don't have to do this. Anyway is it legal?'

'Legal enough,' said the other grimly. 'As legal as that other damned bit o' paper the Cassidys have.'

Corrigan slapped his back. 'Hell, you'll be around to see them Cassidy buzzards light out of this territory!'

'If I'm not, this will give them plenty of trouble,' said Tom Selby, tapping the paper. 'You keep it, Sam. Soon as you can, deposit it with Jedson, the lawyer in town.'

Later in the night they figured to bed down. The fire was kept going, and after some debate Bill Corrigan and Sam Hicks decided to sleep in the wickiup. Bert Foggin and Tom Selby had their bedrools laid out near the fire. Their conversation about cattle and drives, trails and Indians, petered out slowly and was taken place by yawns. The men dropped into sleep. The hills contained a droning sound as small noises of the night took over, like the rustle of wind through some cottonwoods and the idstant howl of a lone coyote.

The dark figure that crept towards the glowing

embers had left a horse securely tethered some distance back. He had a natural inborn ability to move like a shadow and a preference for working at night. His moccasined feet made less noise than the breathing of cattle at night. His dark, worn buckskins made him only a darker patch against the rest of the darkness.

He carried a gun but his hand lay softly against a keen bowie knife.

He came closer and closer to the sleeping men and then he paused. His big bulk made no sound.

Bat Grayson had decided to strike.

Chapter Nine

Sylvia Peek was not surprised when the man known as Ed Hunter presented himself at the school-house door only a moment after she had locked the premises for the night. He had sought her company quite a few times. Being a woman she was flattered and yet she had a strange feeling that this man was a mystery. He was courteous, attentive and drew from her a lot of personal details of her own life, but she really learned little about him in exchange.

'Good evening, Sylvia,' he said. 'Are you finished now for the night?'

'Well, yes. The children have gone home and I have no homework to correct. . . .'

He pointed to the two-wheeled rig and the patient horse. 'Would you like to ride with me for some way?'

There was no way to refuse. She was a kindly girl at heart. She said: 'Well, thank you, that would be nice!'

'So little in West Plains in the way of civilized entertainment,' he murmured. 'The restaurants are rough and the theatre non-existent. Now back east, in Baltimore, a gentleman could take a lady to a fine restaurant. . . .'

'Have you lived in Baltimore?' she asked gently.

He nodded. He seemed to change the subject. 'Bill Corrigan is on his feet again. He's been in town.'

'I was a fool about all that,' she said sadly.

He assisted her into the gig and then climbed aboard himself and took up the reins. The horse high-stepped away down the dusty road, passing a few buildings on the outskirts of the town. Soon they were among the rolling green hills of Wyoming. The sun was slanting down for a blazing rendezvous in the distant cups formed by the hills.

'The men to blame,' he said carefully, 'for your brother's death should be Sep and Clark Cassidy.'

'I'll just have to try and forget,' she faltered. 'I was an absolute fool to hate Corrigan ... or blame him ...'

'You admire him, don't you?'

'I—I—just think he stands up to the Cassidys ...'

Suddenly he showed anger. He flicked the reins. 'I stand up to them, too. . . .' He broke off.

'You? They are your employers.'

'I detest them ...'

'I have realized that—and you also have secret reasons for working for them. You don't need to tell me anything.' She glanced at him coolly. 'You would like to kill them, wouldn't you?'

'Dear Sylvia, you are guessing. . . .'

'But you don't carry a gun.'

He smiled a little. 'There is a slight bulge under my jacket. It is so slight you probably haven't noticed it. I hope you have not. But it is a gun.'

Her dark eyes flashed to his black jacket. 'It isn't noticeable.'

'Good. I'm an office manager—a business man. I'm not a frontier gunman.' He paused and then reined in the horse. The gig rocked to a standstill near a clump of old oaks. With a swift but gentle motion he took the girl's hand.

'Sylvia, I'd better come to the point. The reason I've met you—and will continue to meet you—is this: have I any chance of your affections? Would you consider marrying me?'

It was a courteous proposal, in the manner of the times, and not entirely unexpected, yet she was surprised. She falted. 'I—I—I'm not sure.'

'Naturally, I won't press for an answer now but . . .'

'I don't really know you,' she exclaimed. 'Oh, you are kind and considerate—but you must admit you do not confide in me—I mean—you seem to retain many secrets!'

He nodded. His face was a bit hard. 'Pretty soon I'll be able to explain, Sylvia. I—I take it there is some hope for me?'

'There might be more hope,' she said gently, 'if you'd explain why you hate the Cassidys and yet work for them.'

He nodded again. 'Perhaps I will—in a day or so. I have a feeling it won't be long—before—the—Cassidys —are dead!'

He would not explain and they rode back to town making conversation that was light, pleasant and only entertaining. He took her to a little eat-house run by a widow where they drank tea and ate buttered scones. Still Ed Hunter revealed no more of his motives than he had previously although he seemingly found real pleasure in the girl's company. Then, later, they had to part and Sylvia Peek went back to the family with whom she lodged. Ed Hunter returned to the Gold Nugget. With the air of a man who knows his way around, he moved through the saloon, the card tables and then to an office at the back.

He was very busy for some time looking through legal documents and invoices from many sources. He seemed dissatisfied, however, and he turned to the large safe which was standing against the wall. He took out from his pocket a small key and tried it in the lock, but it would not turn. No matter how many times he attempted to open the safe door, the handle refused to move fully.

He stared at the key for some time and muttered: 'It isn't quite right. Guess it needs more filing . . .'

A noise in the passage made him wheel and the key went out of sight. When Sep Cassidy entered the office, Ed Hunter was reading a letter from a freight merchant.

'You!' said Sep sullenly. 'I thought you were finished for the day.'

'Just checking this letter. There's a mistake in their terms. They're robbing themselves.'

'Let them,' snapped Sep. His wrinkled face stared at the other man. 'I've got news for you, Hunter. Clark

124

and me have been thinking. We don't need your services any longer. Now that we've got strong-arm men like Hogan working for us, we can attend to the business affairs ourselves.'

'This is a bit sudden—' began Ed Hunter.

'Well, everything's sudden!' sneered the other. 'What the hell do you want—a pension?'

Anger flushed into Ed Hunter's face.

'You needn't talk to me like that.'

'I'll talk anyway I like,' came the arrogant reply. 'You see Clark in the morning and he'll pay you off.'

'You two are not in a position to bully me,' said Ed Hunter softly. 'If the bank in Laramie knew the extent of your borrowing from other sources, they might foreclose on the saloon, the Gold Nugget.'

'You'd better watch what you're sayin'!'

'You're riding high,' said Ed Hunter quietly, 'but one push and you might topple.'

Sep Cassidy stared at his employee with new suspicions flooding through a cunning mind. 'You've been spyin'!'

'I know your business affairs—that's all.'

'Clark will handle you,' said Sep uneasily.

'With his Remington Double Derringer in the trick pocket!' flashed Ed Hunter, and then he could have bitten off his tongue.

'What d'you know about that?'

'One observes,' said Ed Hunter and he moved to one side. He walked to the door. 'Good night, Sep. Be seeing you.'

He wanted to get away before the other man, with his low animal cunning, riled him into saying more.

He went into the saloon and mingled with the crowd. The place was doing well, he thought grimly. Cowpokes with the rolling gait mingled with the railroad workers who seldom wore guns. Mule skinners with their tales of stubborn animals and impossible trails talked to lumbermen having a day off from the forests. The two barkeeps were busy setting down the bottles of hooch and mugs of beer and taking in return clinking coins and rustling dollar bills.

The pay-off did not worry him. What did irk him was the sombre fact that he had not accomplished what he had set out to do in West Plains. At least, not yet.

He bought a drink and pondered. Thoughts of the girl, Sylvia, mingled with brooding ideas of vengeance. He wondered how much longer he would maintain his role. The weight of the gun inside his jacket seemed suddenly significant. Perhaps all his scheming would be to no avail and the score would be settled crudely—with a gun.

Out of a corner of his eye he suddenly saw Sep Cassidy in the saloon and he was talking earnestly to Hogan.

The thin gunman in black was smoking a cigar, nodding and listening. Twice he looked over in Ed Hunter's direction. Owing to the angle of the mirrors behind the bar, Ed Hunter could see him, as well as out the corner of his eye. He had no use for Hogan. He was not afraid of him, but only a fool would try to beat the man at his own game. He was a professional. Corrigan, however, had got near to it. . . .

He wondered if the two men were discussing him. Something had got into Sep's grisly mind, some suspicion of him. Could be anything; some little happening—maybe, after all, someone had seen him talk to Corrigan in the alley. Maybe they did not like the fact he had been seen with the girl. Well, the hell with them!

He turned and left the saloon. He went back to the hotel where he had been staying.

He examined the key to the Cassidy safe once more, noted the bright spots where it had pushed hard against tumblers and failed to move them. He went to a little drawer and brought a small file, triangular and only four inches in length, such as a locksmith might use. He got busy and smoothed down the bright spots on the key. After thirty minutes of careful work he was satisfied.

Much later that night he mingled with the drinkers and gamblers in the Gold Nugget again, his black suit not too conspicuous for there were others similarly attired. At a suitable moment he slipped into the passage and went to the office at the back. No one saw him except a couple of drunks, who grinned and waved.

The key worked at first try and for the first time since he had worked for the Cassidy brothers he was able to search the safe. There were numerous business papers, in copper-plate penmanship, and a larger wad of dollar bills of all denominations. Carefully, he went though the papers, many of them recent and of no interest, and then

127

he saw the manila envelope marked simply CHINOOK. His eyes flashed and without even bothering to read the contents of the envelope, slipped it into an inside pocket. He stared at the wad of money, took it out, divided it into two smaller wads and slipped elastic bands over them and carefully slid them into his side pockets and smoothed down the cloth. Then he closed the safe door.

With care he reached the passage and then the saloon. He moved casually. There was no sign of Hogan or the Cassidys. He pushed through the batwings, stared at the shadows beyond the pools of light flung by the oil lamps inside the Gold Nugget. Then he stepped forward, walked quickly along the planks, across the dirt road to the hotel and hired a horse, saddled and ready, from the nearby livery.

He rode carefully out of town, hoping the moon would rise.

Chapter Ten

The shadow crept closer to the fire, paused like some big black predator. The red glow hissed as heat reached some new sappy wood. The regular breathing of the four men added another small sound to the night air. A horse stirred in the corral, hoofs thudding slowly at cold earth. A quarter moon peeped out from behind slow sailing clouds.

Bat Grayson knew his orders. But more important to him was the sullen desire for revenge he was nursing. The ugly emotion lay heavily in his guts and showed in his black glittering eyes. His mouth was twisted from a straight slit to a curl of murderous anticipation.

The sleeping men were just huddled forms, blankets and discarded hats making identification hard. His animal mind had fixed on one conclusion and he would carry it out.

A whole line of savage ancestors had enacted this play at some time in their lives, and the cold lust to kill was a real thing. He was sure that Corrigan was one of the two men sleeping just outside the wickiup, near the fire.

A savage needs to find elation in dealing out death, and Bat Grayson, his Indian heritage overwhelming any other blood, was no exception.

He leaped the last yard, raised the gleaming knife and could not restrain a rasping cry of triumph. The knife sank into the huddled form below him. Twice the blade flashed in the air and struck again. The agonized cry of a man in whom pain has leaped through his whole being, cut the air and brought the others jerking to life.

Bat Grayson flung himself at the other man who had been sleeping nearby, but this man was Bert Foggin and he rolled as the savage shape leaped at him. The terrifying cry of a dying man had stung him into frantic awareness of danger. Bert rolled and the knife tore into his blanket.

Another shape came bounding out of the wickiup, like an avenger from hell.

Corrigan crashed into Bat Grayson and the knife became a focal point of the struggle. Corrigan grabbed the man's arm, felt the strength behind the burst of savagery. He twisted the arm until something nearly broke. The knife fell from fingers that could no longer grip. Bat Grayson twisted and relieved the pressure on his arm. His other hand sought Corrigan's face like a filthy claw and began to gouge at Corrigan's eyes.

The rancher had to jerk back. The terrible hand scraped down his face, drawing blood. Corrigan brought up his knee and rammed it into the other's stomach. Groaning and spitting, the man buckled. Corrigan stepped back and swung two vicious punches that jarred

130

damnably into the mask before him. The blows smashed out a spluttering snarl from the man. He tried to escape by backing and he came close to the fire.

Corrigan was on him remorselessly and all at once they fell, locked together. They hit the burning embers and sparks rose into the night air. Bat Grayson was underneath Corrigan. The man's clothing began to smell like a burning rat. His arms rammed wildly, hitting Corrigan under the chin, knocking his head back. Bill Corrigan pressed down, a red mist of rage impelling him on. The half-breed tried to get free by a sudden jerk. It only brought his face into the red embers. Corrigan held him down and listened to the shriek of pain without any feeling of horror. The man moaned in an awful bass slobber, like the baying of a gutted steer. The smell of burning flesh and hot ash caught Corrigan's eyes and nostrils, but he did not let up.

Then, sudden sick emotions hitting him, her jerked up, heaved the tortured man with him and with a blow sent him crashing to the ground.

Bat Grayson got clumsily to his feet and began to run, arms outstretched like a blind man. His burnt lips spewed unearthly sounds. He took a few staggering steps and then a gun barked.

Corrigan whipped around. Bert Foggin held a smoking Colt. As Corrigan whipped again, Bat Grayson fell flat on his face and lay still.

There was a hellish silence for a few moments and three men stood stock still as if caught in a moment of time that would not pass on. The three seconds seemed to last and last. Then they heard the groan from the fire and they turned and came to Tom Selby and leaned over him and made worthless sounds, three men who could do nothing to save him.

Tom Selby was near to death. Blood pooled out everywhere as if the man's heart was on some mad mission to pump his life away. The two knife wounds had hit deep and only a miracle worker could save him.

There were no miracle men among the three. As they leaned over him, there were no last words from Tom Selby. He groaned and gurgled and stared with glazed eyes. The gates of hell or heaven were wide open and, within a few minutes, he slid through them. Corrigan lowered his body to the ground and put the blanket over his head.

'Hell take it,' he ground out. 'We brought him here for safety and . . .'

'Them Cassidy coyotes!' snarled Bert Foggin. 'Say, that galoot near durned got me!'

'That man must have a horse somewhere out there in the dark,' muttered Sam Hicks. 'I'll go get it.'

Corrigan went to the prone Bat Grayson and turned him over. He was really dead. He dropped the body in disgust. Once again he felt repulsion against this code of destruction that was forced on him. He tramped back to the well in the ranch-yard and hauled up some water. He used it gingerly on his face and hands, winced a bit as cold water hit some burns. He got rid of the sticky bloodied feeling, however, and turned back to the fire and the wickiup as Sam Hicks returned leading a black horse.

'Use that in the morning to git this hombre back to West Plains,' he muttered.

'This should make those Cassidy buzzards mighty sore,' said Sam.

'Tom Selby is dead!' said Bill Corrigan angrily. 'They've hounded him ... killed him. ... Sep and Clark Cassidy are as much killers as that 'breed!'

'Yep. And what about that paper he wrote out,' Sam reminded him. 'If yuh get a judge to rule that as legal, yuh're the owner of the lumbercamp.'

'I don't want—' began Corrigan, and then he paused.

'Yeah,' said Sam Hicks. 'I thought you'd see it. You can beat the Cassidy hombres on this. Judge Hendricks is a fair man, I hear—though I'm just a cowpoke an' never had much dealings with the law.'

'He can't be bought, I'll say that,' said Bill Corrigan slowly. 'An' you're right—this will hit those two carrion where it hurts.'

They sat down close to the fire and stared into the shadows made by the flickering flames. A slip of moon was climbing the night sky and relieved the velvety darkness a bit. Bert Foggin threw more wood on the fire as if in instinctive defiance of the night. They stopped talking, just stared set-faced. Everything had been said it seemed. After the warmth of the day, the night was cold. They shivered and then wrapped the blankets around themselves. They thought they should

133

be sleeping but with two bodies lying around sleep did not come easily.

Bert Foggin and Sam Hicks were the first to drop off. They rolled over as drowsiness overtook them and curled in their blankets. Corrigan sat hunched up, staring, his hat well over his head, the blanket around him, thinking about Tom Selby. He had liked the man. Before the Cassidys had appeared on the scene, Tom had been a jovial friend. No doubt he had had secrets which he had not shared, but that could be said of a lot of men in the frontier towns.

His hatred of the Cassidy brothers welled up again and stuck in his throat. Tomorrow, he thought, with terrible clarity, there would have to be a showdown.

He heard the soft fall of a horse's hoofs from a long way off, as the animal picked a slow careful way along the dark trail. Someone was coming.

Corrigan sat and listened to the sounds for some time and did not waken the other two. He got to his feet and palmed his gun. He walked away from the red glow of the fire and stood in the shadows, the blanket around him, his hat shading his eyes. He waited.

The man who rode out of the night was no killer. The patiently jogging animal brought the man quite close to Corrigan before he realized it. The rider jerked a bit when Corrigan spoke. 'What brings you out here, Mr Hunter?'

'I came to see you, Corrigan.'

'Well? What do you want?'

'Allow me to get down from this saddle first,' said

Ed Hunter. He swung down and walked slowly to the fire. Corrigan took his horse and led it to the corral. When he returned Ed Hunter was staring at the body of Bat Grayson lying prone, face down, some distance away in the fringe of light from the fire.

'Who is that?'

'Bat Grayson. He crept in here an' killed Tom Selby.'

'Selby—is—dead?' Ed Hunter's eyes glinted from under his hat as the firelight caught them.

'Stabbed by that blasted snake,' said Bill Corrigan bitterly. 'Old Bert got him with a Colt.'

'Looks like you've had another fight, too?' said Ed Hunter sharply.

'Yeah, there was a fight.' Corrigan told the other man most of the facts. 'There, Mr Hunter. Death—the final count. I suppose it is the only thing that is really final.'

'There are two men in West Plains who should be dead,' said Ed Hunter slowly. 'Sep Cassidy and his brother, Clark.'

'Yeah—yuh talk a lot, Mr Hunter.'

'You want to know why I'm here?'

'That would be interestin'—so long as it don't take all night,' said Corrigan dryly.

'I've been sacked by Sep Cassidy . . .'

'Hell, is that all?'

'Allow me to continue. I have also been inside his safe—something I've been trying to do for a long time. I've got some papers—which I knew would be there —that will send those two men to prison for a long time. I've also got some compensation for you from the Cassidy brothers for the loss of your ranch buildings and stock.'

He brought out a wad of money and thrust it at Bill Corrigan. Ed Hunter succeeded in astonishing his man. By this time Bert Foggin and Sam Hicks were awake again and grumpily staring at the newcomer.

'Tarnation, can't a man git some blastit shuteye around hyar!' grumbled Bert.

'Always was quiet when we slept in the bunk-house,' muttered Sam.

Bill Corrigan gripped the other man's arm. 'I think yuh might as well sit down, Ed. And tell me the yarn.'

The other brought out the envelope marked CHINOOK. He tapped it thoughtfully for a moment. 'Unless I'm mighty wrong—and I'm sure I'm not—this envelope contains all the details of Sep and Clark Cassidy's business affairs when they were in Chinook, Montana. They were two money-grabbing hardcases up there, I can tell you. They left the town in a hurry and left hundreds of people ruined. Not only that Clark Cassidy killed a man.'

'Someone yuh knew?' probed Corrigan.

'You're beginning to understand. Yes, Clark Cassidy killed my young brother.'

'Why didn't the law get him?'

'The law never found out,' said Ed Hunter harshly. 'I'm the only man who knows—and I doubt if I'll ever prove it. My brother Alan talked to me just before he died. He'd been cheated by the Cassidy brothers—

136

worthless shares in non-existent property—and he had tackled Clark Cassidy.'

'The man doesn't tote a gun!'

'Don't be fooled. He wears a Remington Double Derringer in a trick pocket. Sep doesn't use a gun.'

'Yuh found your brother before he died?'

'Yeah. I learnt enough but the Cassidys had skipped town that night. It took me months to find where they had gone. I secured a job with them as you know—they didn't know me—with the avowed intention of getting revenge. I made investigations and discovered a lot about the Cassidys. Now with this envelope, containing the papers which I think it contains, I can ruin them by setting the law on them. They can be arrested and brought to trial.'

'Nice and legal an' tidy,' said Corrigan.

'That's it.'

'When they should be dead!' snapped Corrigan.

'Yes, they should be dead,' muttered the other.

'They hounded Tom Selby and had him killed. Old Walt, the waiter at the Broken Horseshoe, was as good as killed by them.'

'And my brother Alan!' reminded Ed Hunter harshly. 'Prison isn't good enough . . .'

'I realize that now,' said the man known as Ed Hunter. 'When I contrived to get that job with the Cassidys, I thought to get them legally. After all, I'm not a Colt packing gunny and I couldn't force a fair fight on them even if I was. I've worked to get these papers . . . lied

137

... fooled people ... even changed my name. I'm not called Hunter. My name is Harnwell—Ed Harnwell. I thought the Cassidy brothers might remember that name —so I became Hunter.'

'I'll call you Ed,' returned Corrigan with a thin smile. 'Now about this money—yuh took it from their safe?'

'That's it.'

Corrigan eyed the wad. 'Must be a fair amount.' He began to count. 'Yep. Nigh on a thousand dollars.'

'It will help you buy timber, hire labour to rebuild your ranch.'

Corrigan stuffed the money inside his shirt. 'My moral values git lower every day of this tussle with them Cassidys. Now I want them dead.'

'I do, too!' Ed Harnwell leaned forward. 'I want to back you, Corrigan.'

'Yuh're not a range man. But yuh've asked for trouble, takin' that dinero from the safe. They'll soon connect yuh with the loss of the money.'

'I realize that.'

'Stick around,' invited Corrigan. He laughed grimly. 'I said that to Tom Selby an' now he's dead.'

'I'll stick around. And if I die, it's too bad.'

They sat around the fire for some time and Ed Harnwell read the papers from the envelope marked CHINOOK. He nodded and made some curt remarks as he read.

'Enough here to indict them ... queer how a man will hold on to old documents ... details of property transactions ... payments withheld from legal owners

... ah, yes ... titles to property forged ... and more.'

'No use contacting Dan Holladay,' muttered Bill Corrigan. 'He's sold out to the Cassidys, I guess.'

'These papers will go to the U.S. Marshal at Laramie.'

'How? Yuh aimin' to ride out there?' Corrigan yawned.

'There are trustworthy men who will ride there for a consideration.'

'Waal, yuh got some dinero—Cassidy money!' said Bill Corrigan cynically. 'Hell, I'm tired! We've got to sleep.'

'I shore wish yuh would!' mumbled old Bert from inside his blanket.

'Yeah ... ain't no comforts around here—so hows-about a little silence?' put in Sam Hicks.

Bill Corrigan yawned again. 'Best set yourself near the fire, Ed. Yuh got no blanket nor bedroll.'

'I'll keep watch,' said the other thinly. 'You never know—you might have another visitor!'

He was as good as his word and the night passed without more trouble. The cool morning sun raised its shining light on the horizon, hinting at warmth to follow, and the men on the ground near the dead fire stirred. They faced the light of another day, each with his own thoughts, wondering what the hours might bring. The green hills, lush with grasses brought on by the warmer weather, bore the shadows of scudding clouds and a few hawks wheeled high in the air. The bellow of some distant steers, moving on for water, added evidence that this was a new day.

Bert Foggin had assumed the job of cook and he got the fire going again. With the few bare utensils they had, he cooked a breakfast of bacon and beans and, with coffee, set it before the others with the air of one who has accomplished at least one satisfactory chore. They ate in silence, and when they had almost wiped the tin plates clean Bill Corrigan produced some of the dollar bills.

'Bert—Sam—I'm payin' yuh up-to-date for your time. And addin' bit. It's spendable dinero—and don't ask questions. It's as good as bank money.'

'Better!' cackled Bert. 'I heerd you two last night! Me —I figger a beer in town would be a mighty good idee!'

'Better patronize the Broken Horseshoe,' said Ed Harnwell dryly.

'Hold it,' said Corrigan. 'We might have visitors.'

'Who d'yuh reckon. . . .'

'Sep and Clark Cassidy will be hopping mad when they discover they've been robbed,' said Bill Corrigan. 'An' they could easily figger Ed here rode out thisaway.'

'So?'

'They hire Hogan—an' they can git other hardcases by the day.'

'Yuh think they might ride out here, boss?' asked Sam Hicks quietly.

'Might.' Corrigan turned slowly, his eyes cast down thoughtfully. 'Sam—I wouldn't blame yuh if yuh figured you've got your dough and—er—wanted to ride on.'

He caught the other man's honest eyes grinning. Sam

Hicks said: 'Look, boss, when yuh git this place built up again yuh'll need a top hand. Waal, I kinda like the idee. So I figure to take the good with the bad.'

But Corrigan knew—and the other knew—that there were loyalties which mere words could not sort out. And that went for Bert Foggin, too.

'Later,' mused Corrigan, 'we'll have to visit West Plains. We need an undertaker for Tom Selby an' I want a word with Judge Hendricks. And this buzzard bait, Bat Grayson, can be dumped down on the Gold Nugget steps.'

'I figure to send a rider to the US Marshal at Laramie,' said Ed Harnwell.

Sam Hicks scanned the horizon with shrewd eyes. 'Say, you really think we'll have visitors?'

'Call it a hunch,' said Corrigan.

'I've got that hunch, too,' said Ed Harnwell.

'Just one thing,' said Bill Corrigan. 'A wickiup isn't my idea of a place to hole up. We've haven't got a ranch-house or a barn in which to take cover. So I think we'll mosey over to the big cottonwood clump.'

They placed Tom Selby's body in the wickiup but, on Corrigan's orders, they left the corpse of Bat Grayson where he had fallen.

'I hope they arrive before the buzzards,' said Bill Corrigan unpleasantly.

Chapter Eleven

Sylvia Peek woke up with the glorious knowledge that the school was on holiday that day and she did not have to get up too early and hurry to her duties as school marm. The kids were great but an odd day off had a wonderfully restorative effect.

All the same, being a young girl with a full share of high spirits, she was up and about as the eager sun climbed into the sky. Dressed in a crisp checked shirt and jeans, she decided to hire a horse and ride out to see Bill Corrigan. Now that he was well and active, according to Ed Hunter, she felt she must explain her past conduct once more. She walked to the livery, smiled at some of the astonished glances she got from some older women going to the store. They were not used to seeing a lithe young girl clad like a boy, but this attire was better than riding side-saddle in a skirt. Before she reached the livery she had received glances from passing men—of admiration. One gallant in cowpoke clothes swept off his hat as he passed!

She was leading the horse out of the livery when she

saw the sheriff striding grimly to his office. He came
level with the girl and stopped, his eyes accusing.

'So your friend has turned robber!'

'Who? What are you talking about?' She held the
horse steady.

'Ed Hunter—that's who! Oh, we know yuh been
pally with that gent! He rode out last night, didn't he?'

'I don't know for sure. He—'

'Maybe yuh know somethin' about it!' shrilled Dan
Holladay. 'He rode out with over two thousand dollars
belong to Sep and Clark Cassidy! Do yuh know where
he is?'

'I don't—and I don't believe you.' She backed in
alarm from the wild look on the sheriff's face. It seemed
obvious that this man was losing control of himself and
events and should not be in office.

'You were seen riding' a rig with him yesterday. But
the hell with that! We figure he headed out to Corrigan's place. Yuh want to know why? He's been spyin'!
Mr Cassidy told me. Spyin'! And Corrigan got Tom
Selby to leave the lumbercamp and head to his place—
so we figure Hunter might be there. I'll git that hombre!
He's broken the law! He's a robber! I'm not standing
for that in West Plains!'

'You stand for plenty of other things, Sheriff Hollo-
day!'

He backed away, feeding his anger. 'I don't intend to
listen to yuh, young lady! I got work to do. We're ridin'
out to git that rogue, Ed Hunter!'

He strode away, full of his anger. At that moment he

was full of a justifiable rage. He was the law and he was going to do something about it. That his anger might collapse like a pricked bubble was a factor he shut his eyes to. He stalked into his office and reached for his rifle.

Sylvia Peek got aboard her hired hack and sent it cantering down the trail. She had food for thought. Was this some sort of trick on the part of the Cassidy brothers? Had Ed Hunter really robbed his employers? He was so much of a mystery that she did not know what to think.

The clear spring air clarified her thoughts as she let the fresh horse have its head. She rode fast. She wanted to see Bill Corrigan—and Ed Hunter. For one thing, she could warn them. And another point; she was involved with these two men. One had asked her to marry him. The other? She hardly dared to think about Bill Corrigan. . . .

She kept the livery animal going at full canter because she felt some urgency here. She was sure the sheriff meant business. Maybe he intended to arrest Ed Hunter. Anything could happen, especially if he took along his gunslinger deputy!

She knew she was ahead of any other riders, and she intended to keep it that way. The trail wound through the grassy hills, passing the occasional rocky outcrop. She left the stage trail proper and cut across the green land. She had seen only a freight wagon and two other riders leaving town—and they were strangers—and they stared curiously as she urged her horse to its limits.

When she finally arrived at the Double C the horse was sweating and blowing. She had been noticed, of course, and Ed Harnwell—to use his real name—came out of the clump of cottonwoods which stood a few hundred yards east of the ranch-house site. He walked swiftly to the girl and took her hands.

Bill Corrigan stared. The sight of this dark-haired lithe girl stirred a curiously mixed set of emotions within him, and the sight of Ed Harnwell taking her hands with such obvious concern perplexed him. He shrugged. Why was he wasting time thinking like this? More important, what in tarnation had brought her out here?

He soon discovered her reasons.

'The sheriff is coming out here! He says he's going to arrest Ed—Mr Hunter!'

'Sylvia, I must talk to you,' began Ed Harnwell, and he took her arm and they walked to one side. Bill Corrigan watched them curiously as they conversed for some minutes in a low voice. Then they joined the others near the cottonwoods.

'I've told Sylvia everything,' said Ed Harnwell simply.

'Good,' said Corrigan. 'Saves a lot of yapping.'

'Looks like your hunch was correct. Sylvia says Holladay is coming out to arrest me.'

'That means he'll bring his pal, Hogan.'

'Maybe I ought to ride out,' muttered Ed Harnwell. 'After all, he can make the robbery charge stick.'

'Forget about Holladay. He dances to any tune. Just remember yuh've got plenty to stick on the Cassidys.'

'And Hogan?'

'We'll take care of Hogan.' Bill Corrigan turned grimly and faced down the trail. The green hills and plains lay silent and smiling under the warming sun as if, like himself, waiting events. It was good to live on one's own land, feel the sun and air, and it might be good to die that way—if one had to die. The silent trail, showing bare yellow earth where passing hoofs had worn the grass, seemed to stretch into the unknown. He stared for a long time and then slowly shook off these feelings.

If Hogan showed up he would have to act like a striking rattler—not a dreamer!

But thirty minutes passed and still there was no sign of riders along the West Plains trail. A waiting game was not to Bill Corrigan's liking and he moved restlessly. The others stood around in groups, talking, smoking.

He strode away, a big man with long strides and a sun-tanned face. He wanted to mosey around. He wished he could see more than a few hundred yards down the trail. If only a guy had the powers of observation that would reveal happenings a mile away! But it was like reading another person's mind—it was not possible.

As he stood on a hillock and stared at a distant bunch of steers, wondering if they all bore his brand, he became aware that Ed Harnwell had approached him.

'You don't like a waiting game,' observed the man.

'Nope.'

'I've had to play it so long . . .'

'Sure.'

'Sylvia is a wonderful girl,' said Ed Harnwell unexpectedly. 'I want you to know I've asked her to marry me.'

Corrigan turned and stared. 'Waal, I'm durned! Are yuh the marryin' kind?' He bunched one hand into the other, thoughtfully. 'Did she accept you?'

'She is considering my offer.'

'Yuh make it sound like it was another bit o' business!' said Corrigan dryly. His eyes gleamed. 'Now if I were the marryin' kind o' galoot—which I'm not—I'd ask thet gal nice an' proper—being a western gent—but I reckon I'd take her in my arms and kiss her soon as I'd got the words out. Yessir! That's the way I'd do it!'

'We happen to be different, Corrigan,' said Ed Harnwell stiffly.

'Yup. Sure. Jest tellin' you what I'd do. . . .'

'I'm going back to the others,' said Ed Harnwell abruptly.

Bill Corrigan stood and watched the other depart, and he felt for the makings in his shirt pocket. He rolled a cigarette, lit it and still stared at Ed Harnwell. Some sort of annoyance with the guy clouded his judgement. He just did not look right for that girl. He wondered what sort of man she might marry. Somehow he could not think of a possible suitor. Something wouldn't be right—that girl just marrying anybody. There was something here he couldn't see!

He came down the hill, still thoughtful, smoking, and then realized he had walked close to the girl. He halted.

'Howdy, Miss Sylvia, you havin' a day off from the school?' he muttered.

'Yes. It's a local holiday.' Her dark eyes swept him with real concern. 'Do you feel fit again? I mean, are you sure you should be so active after those wounds. . . .'

'I'm fine.' He smiled. He did not realize it but his smile was a rare thing and when it came the patent honesty of the man showed. His eyes gleamed and white teeth showed behind firm lips. 'Now don't yuh worry about those hellions. We can take care of them. But you shouldn't be here . . . not if there's goin' to be any shootin'.'

'I—I—wanted to see you,' she faltered. 'Just to say how sorry I am about—about the fool way I behaved. Oh, now that I can think clearly—if you'd died in that gun-fight with Hogan . . .' She broke off.

'That's all past,' he said quietly. He squinted into the sun, down the trail. 'Yuh know, Miss Sylvia, I ain't never really had much time to know yuh—not the way I would like—but maybe pretty soon we could ride out together. I'd sure like to show you the boundaries of this spread—that is—' He paused. 'If you ain't a married woman by that time.'

She laughed. 'Married! To whom?' He reddened under his tan and she took pity on him. 'I don't know who I'll marry—Bill—Corrigan!'

She turned and moved away. At that moment Corrigan heard a shout from Sam Hicks.

'Riders! I hear hoof-beats, boss!'

Chapter Twelve

They came down the trail openly and approached the charred remains of the Double C buildings and there they halted, sitting patient horses that had not been hurried. Long before they had arrived in actual sight, Corrigan and his party had hidden behind the cotton-woods some two hundred yards away. They looked out at the three riders.

Three men, two of them unaccustomed to the saddle. Two men had forsaken their scheming and paper-work to ride with the sheriff. Sep Cassidy leaned on the saddle horn and his lined face peered shrewdly from beneath a black stetson. His brother, Clark, sat his horse as if it had been a long time since he had hit saddle leather and he, too, had donned a hat. Seeing them so attired and in the saddle, they looked unfamiliar figures to Corrigan. These two men had always presented an image to him of men who were always indoors, hatless and seated. Their scheming, murderous plans had always been pre-pared behind walls and hired men had done the actual evil work. Now here they were, out in the open. In a swift moment of analysis, he accepted this new image of these two men. There was one thing that jarred instantly into his mind. Where was Hogan?

He thought he knew.

Hogan had been delegated to do the work, and the only suitable employment to a man with twin guns was dealing out death.

Sheriff Dan Holladay gesticulated towards the burnt ranch buildings; then pointed to the cottonwoods. Sep and Clark Cassidy stared. They had seen the horses in the corral, the wickiup and the prone body of the half-breed. They exchanged a few words. Corrigan thought they sat uneasily in their saddles. He waited. The play was theirs.

Sam Hicks and Corrigan had taken the rifles to the stand of cottonwood and Bert Foggin wore his old Colt. If it came to a showdown, Ed Harnwell had his special gun inside his jacket—probably some light Remington. But Bill Corrigan could not see Dan Holladay throwing lead, and certainly not the two men with him. If Clark Cassidy carried a concealed gun, he was the type to use it furtively.

So it figured. Hogan was somewhere, with his twin hoglegs.

'Corrigan!' The inevitable shout came to him. Dan Holladay was still full of righteous indignation. 'Corrigan! We're here to arrest Hunter. He's a robber. He took over two thousand dollars from the Cassidy safe last night. Now you tell him to walk out from them cottonwoods hands up an' real careful.'

Corrigan stepped from behind the broad trunk of the cottonwood.

'Sheriff, yuh can go to hell! Ed here doesn't know anythin' about the money. Yuh tell Sep and Clark Cassidy to prove this allegation. Have they got witnesses? Did they see Ed? How the hell did he git into the safe, anyway? Yuh see, Dan, we don't believe it.'

'I'm the law around here!' Sheriff Holladay's yell made his horse jig. 'I say he stole that money an' I got power of arrest so that we kin have a trial.'

Corrigan turned round and stared behind him, at the knoll of earth some two hundred yards beyond the clump of cottonwoods. He had sensed something. It wasn't a sound. It was impossible to see anything—but the scar on his temple *began to throb*. He turned back again and glared at the sheriff.

'You listen to me. First, Ed Hunter is really Ed Harnwell—an' Sep and Clark ought to remember that name. Second, he's got documentary proof that can send yore two pals to the State hoosegow for a long time. And that's Bat Grayson yuh see lyin' there—dead. He murdered Tom Selby—he's lyin' in the wickiup. Knifed him. But he got his. Old Bert shot him.'

'Yep—I shore did! The skunk!' yelled Bert.

Corrigan walked a bit closer to the three silent, un-easy men as they sat their saddles. 'Cassidy men burnt this ranch. Take a good look, Dan. You got any savvy left in that head o' yours? Or have they bin payin' you? These skunks hired Hogan—and he killed old Walt. They blackmailed Tom Selby—'

151

'I don't want to hear your lies, Corrigan!' Dan Holladay practically shrieked.

'The hell with you—you'll listen! They figured they had Tom Selby over a barrel, but last night before he died he made out a paper—a will—call it a testament—and he left the lumber business to me in the event of his death. I'm not here to benefit by another man's work but I can tell you those Cassidy coyotes haven't a chance in hell of setting their filthy hands to that property. I'll fight 'em every inch o' the way.'

He saw the glances the Cassidy brothers exchanged and the news stung them into speech.

'Corrigan—we're mighty sick of you!' shouted Clark Cassidy. 'You can stand aside and let the sheriff take that thieving Ed Hunter.'

'You won't live long enough to handle that lumber business!' snarled Sep Cassidy. The news had hit him and he was white with rage. 'You're a killer. Sheriff, this man has killed four others—young Al Peek, the Irishman, a young feller up at the lumber camp and Bat Grayson.'

'Hey! I got that snakeroo!' yelled old Bert.

'You hear that, Corrigan?' the sheriff yelled and threw confused glances at some point way behind Corrigan's head. 'Yuh hear that? I reckon you've got to account to the law as well! I guess—'

'Why don't yuh shaddup!' snapped Bill Corrigan. 'You are not the man you once were, Dan! Best thing yuh can do is throw down that tin star and quit—right now.'

'You've got a helluva nerve!' shouted the other in a tremendous fury. 'Wait till my deputy gits you—'

His words tailed off but Corrigan had noted the threat. Once more he turned his head to the grassy knoll and, under tension, felt his scar throb. He walked slowly back to the cotton woods; paused and then bent down and whipped his rifle from the stack at the tree bole. He had not taken his eyes from the knoll where the grasses waved more than ankle high.

As he walked away, Sam Hicks watched him carefully. Old Bert Foggin stared narrowly, then swung unpleasantly to the sheriff and the other two men. Ed Harnwell stood silently watching Sep and Clark Cassidy.

Sylvia Peek felt fear mount inside her as she watched Bill Corrigan walk purposely to the grassy knoll. She had seen this man before rendezvous with danger and she felt more than ordinary concern. She wanted to stop him, take his arm and plead with him to be careful. Maybe this was just being a woman and maybe it was some other emotion. She was not sure.

Corrigan strode on, his eyes narrowed to slits, his gaze fixed on the knoll. Only green grass waved there, so far as anyone could see, but only a few times in a man's life does a sixth sense sting nerves to razor edge sharpness and for Corrigan this was one time. And this was his land, Corrigan's range, as he thought about it, and he'd fight for it and maybe die for it. Danger, he knew, did not lie behind him in the shape of one scared man and two cunning animals. Danger, every sense told him, was right ahead.

He was alone now, a long way out from the cotton-woods which might have given shelter. He did not want shelter. He wanted to fight. All the same, he knew he was a dark shape against the fresh green grass.

Squinting into the sun, he knew it figured. Sure, that was where his enemy would be—with the sun on his back. Choosing the time and the place. Skill and confidence with a gun—sure. But just that little extra to tip the balance. A man did not shoot quite so good with a bright morning sun glowing right into his eyes.

Still Corrigan walked on, slowly, because speed at that moment was not needed. He pulled his hat down a bit more and decided it took the edge off that old sun.

Then he halted.

'Hogan!'

Because the other was playing it easy, nothing moved and no answer volleyed back. Then, imperceptibly, a bit of black showed around the edge of the green knoll. A moment later the tall thin shape of the gunman came into view. He took two or three steps and halted. He was looking down at Corrigan and his thin body, clad in black, seemed very tall. Height gave this man a sinister appearance.

Corrigan eyed the twin guns. His temple had stopped throbbing because the skin was so taut with tension as to have no feeling. He had known those guns bark before. He felt no fear; just an extraordinary sense of total awareness.

He dropped the rifle.

The dark thin shape did not move.

154

'Why wait, Hogan?' called Corrigan softly.

His voice drifted to the other man against the thinner sound of rustling grass.

Still the tall thin man in black did not move. His face was in shadow, something he knew well enough.

Corrigan thought the sun had crept another fraction of an inch higher, which was all to the good. His hat just cut the dazzle out.

And then, like the strike of a rattler, the man on the hill was clawing for guns and his black shape was bending with the speed of his draw.

Corrigan did not know he was matching every second of the other's speed, beating the twin guns with his jabbing right hand, triggering a split second faster than the other. He did not know because his actions were faster than his thought. At least, conscious thought. The second of time expanded to a lot of living and during it he saw the thin black shape buckle, heard the bark of guns and the hiss of slugs as they cut air close to his face.

And then the tall man in black slowly doubled up. The twin guns seemed to drop in a kind of slow motion. Another inch—and one more inch—and Hogan's knees were on the ground. Corrigan stared with crinkled face at this second-consuming pantomime, hardly believing that the scene was real. Hogan was dying. Slowly. And without guns. Because the guns were in the long grass. The skill that made them living things was vanishing from this world.

And then the gunman rolled over and lay flat in the

long grasses, arms outstretched. He looked like a black cross surrounded by green.

The tingle of taut nerves was still within Bill Corrigan and he holstered his Colt with a swift movement.

He turned to walk back and at that moment he heard a shout which seemed to come from Sam Hicks. He was not sure because he whipped around simultaneously with the shout. He heard the rapid tattoo of a horse's hoof-beats. Then the gun cracked. The slug missed him. Corrigan began running and firing at the rider. It was not easy to take aim.

There had been another man behind the grassy knoll with Hogan and now he was riding out, probably scared, and shooting wildly. His horse plunged down the slope, towards the sheriff and the other two men. His intention seemed to be to join them, as if there was safety in numbers. He was not a very experienced gunny. Evidently he had wanted to side with Hogan, probably come out shooting when Corrigan stopped a slug. It had not happened like that and he had lost his nerve.

Bill Corrigan snapped off two shots at the fleeing man which just made holes in the air. All at once guns were barking everywhere. As Corrigan ran back to the cotton-woods, he saw that Sam Hicks was using his gun, firing at the rider who had appeared from behind the knoll.

Bert Foggin added to the cracking noise of Colt fire. In sheer nervous reaction Dan Holladay triggered his gun at the cotton woods, creating a senseless barrage of noise because his horse reared in fright and his slugs simply hissed through the air.

Ed Harnwell took the chance that was presented to him amid this sudden gun-play. His hand slid to his arm-pit and his gun came out.

He wanted it to end this way with death coming to the two men who had killed his brother. All the months of secret hating and scheming seemed to harden into one implacable fact. He wanted Sep Cassidy and his brother dead—so dead that there would be no more thinking about them, wondering how to hurt them. Death would be the final blow and this was the moment to deal it.

He saw the Cassidys wheel their horses and try to control them as the animals, unaccustomed to guns, jigged in fright. Ed Harnwell came out of the cotton-wood clump, his eyes hard and burning. The gunfire had no effect on him. He wanted to be closer to his victims. Now that the moment of total revenge was his for the taking, his gun hand was steady as a rock. He walked quickly towards the sheriff and the Cassidys as they sat jerking, rearing horses.

The other rider galloped his mount to the rear of the three men and then turned and emptied his gun. He hit nothing but dust. Grit spurted up all around Ed Harnwell. He walked on, raised his gun, held it like a man on a target range who has plenty of time to score a bullseye.

He fired as Dan Holladay and the Cassidy brothers were turning their mounts in order to retreat. For Sep and Clark Cassidy this confrontation had not gone to plan and was, indeed, a horror to be avoided. They had not intended to be part of a shooting party. That had been left to Hogan and his hired side-kick. They had been so confident that Hogan could handle the job that they had not considered what might happen if he died.

Fear gripped Sep Cassidy as he clung to his frightened horse. He cursed. He wondered why he had gotten into this.

Clark Cassidy knew there was danger but he thought the horse would get him safely away. He dug heels to its flanks.

Ed Harnwell's first shot hit Sep Cassidy in the shoulder. The man cried in pain and swayed in the saddle.

The second shot from the Remington came a second later and tore a hole right through Sep Cassidy's back, hitting the spine. Those horse leaped and its rider toppled from its back.

Then the man who wanted revenge was firing at Clark Cassidy, holding the gun level with his shoulder. The weapon barked once, twice.

Clark Cassidy took the two slugs square in his back. He seemed to freeze with sudden pain and then, unable to balance in the saddle, he slid sideways. His feet left the stirrups and he hit the ground.

Ed Harnwell was not finished.

The sheriff and the other gunman were riding in fear away from this place of sudden death and the firing had faded away. Ed Harnwell walked up to the two prone men.

Corrigan could not stop him, short of shooting him

down, and that decision was too hard to make in three fleeting seconds.

Ed Harnwell had two more shots left in his gun. He used them. He stood over one dying man and fired into his head, bringing instant death. With a swift leap, Ed Harnwell came to the other man and sent the last slug into his head.

It was an execution. As silence descended on the land, Ed Harnwell stared at his gun and then dropped it. He walked back to the others, slowly eyes on the ground.

Haggard lines had set deeply around his mouth. He stared at Corrigan and the others.

'I had to do it . . . they killed my brother . . . it was the only way . . . after all. . . .'

'But they weren't using guns!' grated Bill Corrigan.

'I've killed them,' said the other with finality.

'There's a helluva lot to answer for!' snapped Corrigan. 'Don't you realize that?'

Ed Harnwell looked at the girl as she came closer with slow footsteps and a look of horror on her face.

'Sylvia—' he began and stopped.

He saw the answers in her dark eyes, now wide with fear and in the way she held Corrigan's arm. She stared at him with a mixture of pity and apprehension.

'Sylvia,' he began again, and then his mouth twisted. 'I'm riding out,' he mumbled. 'Nothing for me here.'

'We can't stop you,' said Bill Corrigan quietly. 'Get your horse and go. Just one thing, Ed—I'll put the facts before the U.S. Marshal. He can figure it out. This is a hard land, Ed, and justice is rough.'

'It's hard,' said Ed Harnwell, 'but maybe I'll find some peace a long way from here. So long, Corrigan. Good-bye, Sylvia. . . .'

He stumbled away to his horse, head down, his shoulders hunched.

When he had disappeared down the trail, Bill Corrigan turned grimly to the scene around him. He met Sam's eyes. He looked at Bert Foggin; even the oldster was subdued.

'We've got some clearing up to do.' Corrigan felt the girl take her hand away from his arm. He looked down into her deep dark pools of eyes. He said: 'I liked the feel of your hand . . .'

'I—I—was afraid!'

He walked her away and slid an arm around her shoulders. 'Yuh needn't be afraid, Sylvia. We've won some of out battles. I don't mean just killin' men . . . though some of them had to go . . . I mean we've kinda sorted out some of the problems inside us. . . .'

'I have,' she said.

'An' me, too! That money Ed took—I'm sending it to some charity. I don't want it. I'm building up this spread in the future. And I hope to God I'm done with killin'! And Sylvia—say, let's git away from those two ornery galoots! There's things I want to say to you an'——well, I don't want them around!'

She smiled and walked with him.